SURRENDERED VI

BY

Peggy Patrick

ISBN-10: 099629595X
ISBN-13: 978-0-9962959-5-6

Cover Design by Charlene Raddon
http://cover-ops.blogspot.com

This book is dedicated to these special people in my life who have gone beyond the call for me in my writing endeavors. My sincere thanks to all of you for your input in my Surrendered series. I could not have gotten this far without you.

Cathy Brown
Amber Cason
Beth Cox
Doris Lillard
Marcia Massey
Sue Neihart
Cody Patrick
Lisa Patrick Sandmann
Jan Scivally

SURRENDERED VI

A surrendered will brings knowledge of truth.

CHAPTER ONE

He felt like a fool—the pain so intense, he could feel a huge fist buried to the hilt in his gut. It had been stuck there for a week now, since the moment she told him she was moving and then broke up with him in almost the same sentence.

Andy Parker had known Abigail Luke since before elementary school. They'd played in the same sand-box, sharing a brother-sister relationship through the years and enjoyed dozens of horse riding adventures on every square inch of High Point Dude Ranch and on her family's Double OO Ranch. They had done this hundreds of times over the years—rode out to a little swimming hold in the creek to picnic and swim, many times with parents and sibling in tow.

Until that day, a year ago, when it was just the two of them at the creek. Something happened.

They sat side by side on a flat rock where the water cascaded over it and created a gentle waterfall off the slab and into the pool. He watched trickles of water drip onto her cheeks from wet, blonde, curly strands and couldn't seem to look away. When she caught him staring at her, she didn't look away either or even smile. Then he slowly learned forward and kissed her. She liked it and they kissed a lot after that.

Over the next months, they spent all their time together—movie dates, riding and working various jobs together for the dude ranch.

Abigail was Andy's first real love interest. He'd had a few dates here and there, but Abby was the only one he ever wanted to be with.

Right now, he wanted to hit something or scream. Or cry. He felt the tears gathering, thankfully blurring the spot in the creek where he had first fallen in love. He stood against a big pine that helped shelter the private little swimming hole on the Double OO and for the first time since she left, he cried.

It had been a long, hot day and Les Kane, the Double OO's long time foreman, walked his gelding slow, guiding him beneath every shade tree as he made his way from the far back side of the ranch. His crew of hands had already made it back to the barn and headed to High Point for supper.

Hank Walton cooked for the two neighboring ranches twice a day from his chuckwagon. His breakfast and supper fixins kept his cowboys happy, so the five-mile trip twice a day was one of the better deals Judd Luke had made for his crew.

Les and his wife, Kaitlyn, rode over occasionally to eat with them, but most times she was already cooking when he got up before daylight and when he dragged himself back in at night. He had no idea what he was getting for supper tonight, but he knew he was starved and he knew it would be good.

He smiled at the thought of his wife. The woman loved him and made no bones about it. The last fight they'd had was before they were married some fifteen years ago. She seemed to just roll with the flow of life, happy to be here. He almost joyously laughed out loud thinking of her, but in that instant, his exhausted pony stopped abruptly, ears perked. Les heard it too, like a muffled cry on the breeze. He looked up from the valley floor toward the high embankment where Judd kept a large tent that occasionally served as a line shack. He listened intently and heard it again—probably the slight wind whistling through a tree, but curiosity had him.

He reined Billy toward the sound and after he reached the summit, another horse snuffled a greeting to Billy from the pen beside the tent. It was Sugar Beet, Andy Parker's horse. His saddle was sprawled carelessly on the ground outside the gate.

Les dismounted, dropped his reins to ground-tie and loosened the gelding's cinch a notch.

He had heard about Andy and Abby's breakup that happened just before she loaded up and moved off to a university. Apparently, she didn't tell him she'd been accepted there until time for her to leave. No one really knew—it all happened so fast. Judd explained that she wanted to get some summer classes out of the way before the fall semester.

Les hadn't seen Andy since all that came down, but it was plain to everybody how he felt about Abigail, and he figured *this* was about *that*.

"Andy?" He called toward the closed tent.

No answer.

He figured it might be best if he just rode on and left him alone—then the same sound came again, but from out behind the tent. He walked that direction a few yards until he caught a glimpse of Andy sitting on the ground against a tree, his hands covering his face.

He went back to the tent and tied the flaps back to create a large open, airy space inside. He busied himself making coffee—and waiting.

Les Kane knew full well what Andy was going through. His wife, before she was his wife, had ripped his guts out by hitting him in the face with the engagement ring he'd given her, because of a horrible mistake he'd made. He had spilled a shot of horse wormer and allowed her family's dog to lick it up. The pup died quickly. He intended to clean it up, but got distracted—a few minutes too long. He hadn't been a licensed veterinarian very long when that happened and he couldn't rationalize the losses—the pup and then Kaitlyn. He left his practice and the state of Missouri within hours and spent the next three years cowboying for Judd Luke, keeping to himself and refusing to forgive himself for his failures.

When Kaitlyn showed up in Wyoming looking for him, he'd come close to blowing it all again.

But God!

He thanked God for being real and alive and for loving his sorry butt every day since.

It was a full hour before Andy's long legs sauntered around the corner of the tent. He knew Les was in there. He'd seen Billy and smelled coffee strong enough to wake the dead from the previous century.

"Evenin." He stepped inside the tent.

"Andy."

"You guarding something tonight?"

Les poured a mug full and handed it to him. "No. Just thought you might need a friend. Or at least a shot of my *heads-up* brew."

Andy took a sip and sat down on a canvas fold–out stool. "Whew…this stuff would grow a mustache on a baby in under three minutes."

Les laughed. "Foreman's trick of the trade—keeps my cowhands' wide awake." He sat back down on another stool.

"Saw Sugar Beet penned when I was headed home. I figured you were soaking in the swimmin hole. Thought I'd make us a shot of coffee. Haven't seen you in a while."

Andy stared hard at the older cowboy. "So, how much did you hear?"

He stared at the ground a few seconds. "Enough to know you're going through a rough time. Just wanted to help some way."

Andy rested his elbows on his spradled legs, both hands wrapped around his coffee cup and stared at the same ground a few seconds. "I appreciate this, Les. I guess I'm not handling

10

this too well. Here I am, an ordained preacher of God's Word and I can't even…"

"Whoa, now." Les paused to think before he spoke. "Andy, you're a man first…a human being who's had his heart jerked out of place. Hurts like the devil. Those are not going to be the last tears you shed, son. Some cuts just take a while to stop bleeding."

"I really thought we had something serious going for us." He shook his head. "She didn't even seem bothered by the fact that she wouldn't see me for a long time—like next Christmas."

"Well…Andy…I know it feels like you'll never feel happy again, but…well, you know as well as I do that when God closes a door, He has a new one He wants to open. Give it some time."

Les felt like he was sitting there lying through his teeth. His breakup with Kaitlyn all those years ago was still a clear memory, not closed behind a door. But, his second chance with her *was* a new door. Maybe Andy and Abby would get another chance together. But, he couldn't make himself say that. Who could say what God's will is for these two-young people?

"I'm supposed to preach a message at church for Judd tomorrow. I don't think I can do it." He looked up at Les. "I can't."

Les looked tired, but not particularly concerned about Andy's declaration that there wouldn't be anyone to hold Cowboy Church services for the more than four hundred people who came out every week. The church building was only around five years old, the property gifted by Andy from a two-hundred-acre inheritance he'd received from his dad, Matthew Parker.

God had made Himself known to Andy as a very young boy, leading him to earn an online degree from a Bible college when he was only twenty. His first desire, as far back as his memories went, was to please his Heavenly Father. But, right this minute, he couldn't stand up and talk about God when he felt so abandoned by Him.

Les nodded. "Then you shouldn't, Andy. You need some down time. I'll handle the service tomorrow.

A weight lifted off his mind at Les's offer. He'd heard him teach an impromptu Bible study around a campfire one night during an overnight cattle roundup. "Thank you. I...appreciate that a lot."

Both stood at the same time.

"Let me practice on you right quick." Les clasped his hand over Andy's broad muscled shoulder and prayed for him.

Afterward, Andy drained his cup and reached for Les's empty one. "I'll clean up in here."

"Nope, this is my mess. Best get saddled. It's already nearly too dark to see. I'll be right behind you."

Andy saddled up and headed out, crossing a few yards in front of Les and Kaitlyn's log home, foreman's quarters for the Double OO. Kaitlyn was sitting on the front porch steps, undoubtedly watching for her husband.

Not willing to fake his way through polite conversation, he stuck his hand up and waved, then jerked his thumb in the direction he'd just come from. "He's right behind me."

She waved. "Hey, Andy. Thanks."

Five miles cross country later, he put Sugar Beet in a stall with an extra handful of grain and managed to get showered and to his bedroom without encountering conversation with anyone.

Sleep came almost immediately, but not before he'd made a decision for himself that he knew was long overdue.

Les led Billy the last few steps to where his wife now stood in the front yard. He walked into her outstretched arms and kissed her, then wrapped his free arm around her in a tight hug.

"I saw Andy ride by a little while ago."

He nodded. "We had some coffee and conversation in the tent. I'll tell you about it after I get this tired boy to bed."

Billy slung his head up and down in agreement. They both laughed.

"Be back in fifteen minutes. And, by the way, I'm preaching tomorrow, God help us."

"Oh, well, it's a good thing Judd asked you to be prepared. We'll talk later. I'll get supper ready."

He kissed her again.

"Yes, I'm positive, Mom." Andy knew this wasn't going to be easy, but everything inside of him was compelling him to go.

He'd told Anna Leigh and Jesse, Jr. good-bye before they left for school, but left out the fact that he didn't know when he'd be back.

"I know your heart is hurting, son. You need to give it a little time."

"Mom, I'm twenty-three years old and still living off you and Dad." He backed up against the kitchen counter and folded his long arms across his chest, one long, slender, jean clad leg resting over the other.

Laura Brandon knew, because she knew her son, there was nothing she could say to change his mind. He was ready to step fully into his adulthood—to cut the last apron string. Her desire to hold on to him was so strong she could taste it. But, she knew that was just the pain of the cutting loose. Andy was a man who stood six feet two inches—independent and fully capable of taking care of himself.

"I understand your need to find your own life, honey. I just hate that you're going off in this state of mind. You don't have a…a destination, do you? Shouldn't you at least have a…a plan of some kind."

She was losing her composure until Jesse's arm came around her shoulders and reined her in with a tight squeeze, soothing her as his fingers kneaded her upper arm.

13

Andy stood up straight, then stepped to his mom and pulled her into a tight, quick hug. His hand went out to shake Jesse's hand, but he was grasped into a group hug.

"Son, you call your mother in a decent length of time when you get somewhere to do it. Gettin' my eggs fried for me again depends on it."

Andy chuckled. Leave it to his dad to smooth out the rough spots.

"I will. Don't worry. Me and God's got this." He didn't know that God was in this, but he said it for his mom's sake.

No, he didn't have a destination or a plan—only a driven need to get away. His late model, three quarter ton pickup was loaded with a dozen changes of clothes in the back seat and plenty of grain and hay under tarps in the truck bed. His two-horse slant carried Sugar Beet and all his roping gear. What else could a cowboy need?

Judd was due to fly back in a day or so after driving with Abby to her college. There were more than enough hands now to handle the dude ranch activities. This move seemed to be in the cards. Or maybe this would turn out to be the dumbest thing he'd done yet. Right this minute, he didn't care how it turned out. He was hurting—he was angry—he'd never felt so far away from God.

He *did* recognize, as he drove his rig out the front gate and onto the highway, he suddenly felt an extreme peacefulness wave through his whole body and mind. Some things were hard to understand—so he didn't try. He just drove.

***

CHAPTER TWO

Summer Logan swallowed at the lump in her throat and repeated for the umpteenth time today—"Thank You, dear God, for feeding me and the girls today."

It had been much easier a few weeks ago to confess to God that she believed and trusted the words in His Holy Bible—the ones that promised He would supply all her needs and that He would never leave or forsake her. But of late, she found it harder to truly believe that, as the days passed.

When she noticed her eldest daughter, five-year-old Emma Jo, looking hard at her through the back-screen door, she forced a wide-eyed smile to cover her fear and spoke as chipper as she could fake.

"Emma Jo, run out and see if the ladies laid us a couple eggs while I whip up a few biscuits for supper. And take Rachel with you. Don't let the hens peck her."

"Okay, Mama. Come on, Rachel, let's get eggs." Emma Jo stepped off the back porch and waited to help her three-year-old baby sister down the eight-inch drop.

"Mama, we get eggs," Rachel chirped as she reached for her sister's hand.

Saying she idolized her big sister was a mild telling. Little sister never let her sibling out of her sight, so there wasn't a chance that Rachel wouldn't tag along to the chicken coop. But Summer said that to remind her five-year-old to keep an eye on her.

Please let there be eggs.

She turned to the task of making a few small biscuits with what was left of the tightly sealed canister of self-rising flour. Billie was still giving enough milk daily to give the girls a fresh warm glass each morning and enough for bread and a little gravy. The hens were laying again after the just passed mild winter. But—this was it. The last of everything she could scrape up to feed her family was gone.

Summer Rain Logan became a single mother after her husband died just over a year ago while the family was shopping in the nearest little mountain town of Forest Valley, Idaho. The horror of that day was still too fresh in her emotions and to make that worse, she had made a bad decision shortly after that, bringing her to the predicament she was in today.

This ancient cabin on the backside of nowhere, twenty miles from the nearest town was Summer's first real home. She'd been raised homeless except for a couple of short stints in foster care when the police took her from the old minivan her parents lived in. She had run away both times, not because the foster family was mean to her—She just missed her mama. After running the second time, her dad drove the van three counties over and no one bothered them there.

Her mama had been her salvation—teaching Summer to read when she was five or six. She remembered working almost every day in school workbooks that her mom got from somewhere. Her mom was smart and pretty, but, there were a lot of drugs around. She ignored that part as much as possible. She never went hungry. Life was just—what it was.

Then Joe Logan walked up to the van one day just before she turned seventeen and introduced himself. Her parents were off somewhere for the night and Joe sat down on the back where the van hatch was open and they talked most of the night. He was funny and thirty years old and thought she was pretty. One month later, they knew they were in love and married in the office of the Justice of the Peace.

Joe had told her about his cabin up in the Sawtooth mountains and how isolated it was, but all she really heard was *cabin. Isolated* was irrelevant.

They had loaded his old smokin', rattlin' truck down with lots of imperishable groceries and cans of gasoline, motor oil and kerosene and miscellaneous stuff he said they had to have to survive decent.

He had bought her new jeans and boots and under clothes the day after they married. She felt like a princess moving to her very own castle with the prince himself.

And their life together was close to a fairy tale. They spent three years getting to know each other before Emma Jo came along. The old cabin was a patched-up mess, but it had a roof and four rooms—more than Summer had ever had in her life. They burned wood to cook and kerosene lanterns for light after darkness fell and snuggled under mounds of pretty quilts on the long winter nights.

Joe had an old generator that kept a small refrigerated box cold when it was needed. The fact that this little world of Heaven was twenty miles from civilization, deep in the Sawtooth Mountains didn't really register as a strange or hard way to live. She had lived the hard way in the back of a minivan.

Joe taught her how to navigate daily life the easiest way and taught her about God and prayer. She prayed one night to be saved and somehow, inside herself, she knew she was His child. Joe taught her how to praise and worship the Lord. They would go outside sometimes and shout how much they loved Him and thank Him for loving them. They would raise their arms high, twirl round and round, dancing in praise to God, before dissolving in hysterical, joyous laughter in each other's arms.

That memory brought a smile to her face now, almost to the point of a giggle as she flattened six small biscuits, deciding to fry them.

"Mama, you're happy again!"

She wheeled around, unaware of the twinkle in her eyes. Emma Jo was beaming up at her, holding three large eggs in her shirt front.

"Mama happy gin," little Rachel mimicked from just behind her sister.

The ear to ear, wrinkle-nosed grin that was spread across her baby's face brought out Summer's suppressed chuckles. She was surprised at how good it felt to expel real laughter again. Her laughter and smiles had all been forced for her babies' sakes— ever since the day their beloved husband and father left them. Her children were obviously not fooled.

She'd had to apply for government funds to bury him. Thankfully a little Church of the Saints in Forest Valley offered interment free of charge in their small cemetery beside the church building. She moved through a haze of shock during those days, thankful that the towns people were so generous to help her.

A confusing mixture of the joyful memory of dancing before the Lord with her Joe and remembering the day he dropped to the floor in the aisle of the grocery store in sudden death, ended with a wave of fresh grief washing over her.

She lowered her eyes to the eggs in Emma Jo's shirt and reached for them, ashamed that she couldn't stay happy for her girls. Sooner or later she would have to stop grieving. These two babies deserved that from her.

After filling them up on one and a half scrambled eggs each and the tiny flat biscuits, she helped the girls say prayers and tucked them in.

It was almost dark. She boiled a few coffee grounds, enough for one cup and picked up the one little biscuit that was left over. The temperature outside had dropped, as usual after sundown and in minutes she had a fire blazing in the fireplace. That served for lighting so she could preserve the dwindling kerosene.

Joe had enough wood cut and split to last for two or three winters—a whole shed full. He usually hauled a load to town and sold it, sometimes working for the feed store a few hours during the trips when he went alone.

She mostly stayed home after Rachel was born. There just wasn't room for all of them in the single cab pickup and there was only one child's car seat. She was perfectly content to stay home and cook and play games with the girls. It was a normal life, for a change, and there just wasn't anything she cared to complain about.

The flames and sparks from the split pine logs were hypnotizing as she concentrated on them and gently rocked in the only new piece of furniture in the house. Joe had purchased the rocker for her just before Emma Jo's birth.

She'd had a decision to make soon after Joe's death. It was obvious that she made the wrong one, because now her two babies were in danger of starving.

Town was too far away to walk with her children. The old truck quit running after her last trip in for groceries several weeks ago. Joe had always had to mechanic on it to keep it going, but that wasn't something she had a clue about. Now they were stranded up here with most all their food staples and other supplies gone.

There was still a little money left from the collection that the church pastor took up for them. She stretched it thin on groceries, but what was left wasn't doing any good with no way to get to town.

It crossed her mind to pray, but she couldn't force another word up to God. He wasn't listening to her.

Hot tears blurred the pretty fire she'd built up. Maybe she should have accepted Wilbur Canton's offer for her and the girls to move into his apartment above the feed store he owned. But he lived there and he wasn't moving out. Something about Wilbur didn't feel right so she lied and told him she was moving away to live with her parents. She didn't want him showing up at the cabin. He had a bad look in his eye that scared her.

But now, she was trapped here with two little ones looking to her for their very lives and she didn't know if she could save them. And, she didn't know right this minute if God was even real.

***

CHAPTER THREE

Andy was plain disgusted. Normally, he didn't mind a side trip to no telling where when he made a wrong turn, but this was ridiculous!

He had rodeoed all over the western half of the country, his roping winnings paying his way to the next one. Sugar Beet was in great form, seeming to be enjoying the rodeo trail as much as he was.

It was going on four months since he'd left home, crossing the south through Colorado, Arizona, back up through Nevada and Oregon—somehow winding up on a cow trail of a mountain road in Idaho. He had driven for miles with no place to even turn around. It was pitch black dark and getting colder as he went, which meant he was obviously headed up a mountain.

That last little town he'd come through, Forest Valley, was ten or fifteen miles back and he hadn't spotted any form of civilization since. He didn't stop for supper, but he thought he had a few slices of bread and a jar of pimento cheese in his cooler from a few days ago. If a town didn't hit the horizon soon, at least he wouldn't starve.

Andy didn't spook easily, but something was more than a mite off beat about the road he was on. Actually, he didn't recall turning off the main highway that ran through the small town. He just suddenly realized he was on this lame excuse for a road and it was completely dark except for his headlights. He *knew* it was still light in the town not ten minutes ago.

He glanced at the clock on the dash of his dually and his breath caught in his throat. More than an hour had passed—not ten minutes. He clearly remembered glancing at the time as he was leaving town.

"This is crazy," he whispered at the windshield. "Lord, I hope You know where I'm at, cause I sure don't."

Immediately he recalled to mind a story his mom had told him a couple years back. She had been driving home from shopping in Jackson, the city in her rear-view mirror, when she found herself driving through the ranch gate an instant later. That was twenty-five miles that she didn't recall driving. She said God had *transported* her over that stretch of road for some reason. And sure enough, a bad head-on collision involving a drunk driver had occurred at the same time she would have been on that highway. She thought maybe she was being spared involvement in that wreck. He had tried hard to believe her, and right now, two years later—he believed her—because *something* weird was happening to him now.

Sugar Beet was due to unload and stretch his legs, but Andy didn't see this as a safe place to do that. Bears or wolves could be out in these woods and chasing a scared horse through this heavy wooded blackness would be fruitless—Maybe deadly.

Abby Luke popped into his mind suddenly. He hadn't thought about her in a few weeks. So, why now? He recognized that the heartache that always came when he thought about her, wasn't there. Maybe it was truly time to move on.

Just then, an easiness seemed to fall over him, like a silky covering wrapping his body. He felt something drain away from his insides. The angry pain he'd been holding on to just oozed out and left him with that *peace that surpasses understanding* that the Bible speaks of. He knew it well, just not since leaving home. He also recognized this as his moment to be able to repent of these past months since Abby broke his heart.

He stopped his rig and threw it in park, immediately dropping his forehead onto the steering wheel.

"My Father...my Father...forgive me. Forgive my rebellion against You these past months. I can't stand feeling so distant from You. Help me, Lord."

He didn't realize he was crying until he raised his head a couple minutes later and tasted the salty wetness that ran across his lips. He swiped his eyes and rubbed his itchy black stubbled face with both hands—sucked in a deep, full breath and then yawned.

Exhausted was a mild way of saying how he felt this minute. If it wasn't for Sugar Beet needing to get out of the cramped two-horse trailer, he would have laid his seat back and slept. In fact, he was so tired now, he couldn't seem to think what to do next.

Rum-dumb, he sat there for maybe two minutes staring in front of his truck as far as the headlights let him see. Only after his whole rig began to rock by an impatient four-legged roping buddy, was he able to sit up straight and force another prayer.

"What now, Lord?"

DRIVE

He put it in gear and drove on, but no further than a quarter of a mile when he spotted a cabin. It was only a blur out of the corner of his eye, but he saw enough to know there was some kind of shelter just off the road a few yards.

He braked and slowly backed until a driveway, of a sort, opened through the trees. His headlights raked over an old half-standing shack and as the driveway curved slightly, his lights landed on a barn that looked better than the house. An equally antique pickup was parked between the two buildings. The place appeared deserted, but it might serve to rest his pony for the night.

With his lights on the front of the closed double doors, he got out and carefully pulled them open, surprised to see hay bales stacked against the wall just inside—maybe a hundred or more. Buckets, ropes, a yard rake and shovel were laying a little further in. He guessed someone could be living in that hovel, but it was so dark and quiet, he opted to take his chances and stay here until morning. *Maybe* he wouldn't wake up shot.

He found a clean stall and unloaded his horse after hanging his own buckets for grain and water along with a good block of hay from the back of his truck.

He first thought he would catch a few winks in the truck, but really wanted to stretch his weary body out straight. The thick loose hay around the bales in the barn appeared soft and clean enough. He threw his heavy duty sleeping bag on the hay, wadded a blanket for a pillow, and after shutting off his truck engine and lights, he stretched out and was sound asleep in no more than twenty seconds.

The blood curdling scream was ear piercing and not far away. It belonged to a very young child.

Andy stirred and turned over, rolling his sleeping bag tighter around himself.

Another piercing scream.

He opened his eyes, squinting into the faint glimmer of dawn that he could see through the half open barn door. Once his eyes focused, he realized he was staring into the eyeballs of a little girl not six inches from his own face.

"Mister, I think your horse wants you."

Andy was sure his entire body had flopped a foot off the ground before he managed to sit up with the ground under his butt.

The noise that woke him up came again from outside where it was still mostly dark, but the scream was now hysterical crying.

Instinctively, he jumped to his feet, raced past the girl who was squatted down by his bedroll and ran outside to rescue whoever belonged to the sobs.

Another girl, about half the size of the first one stood out in the open about half way between the barn and the back side of the old shack. Without a thought, he quickly strode to her and scooped her up, not sure if something was getting her from the ground. She was barefoot, wearing a long-sleeved ankle length washed-out gown. He rubbed a hand over both of her freezing feet and scanned her all over, not finding a problem, but realized she'd stopped crying and was staring at his face like there was something real ugly about it.

"Are you, all right?" He spoke as soothing to her as his jabbering heart would let him.

She puckered. "Emma."

"Is your name Emma?"

"No," came the older voice behind him. "I am and she just wants me. That's why she's crying."

"Mister! —you put my baby down right now and get away from my girls."

He froze, his eyes wide and slightly angry at the sight of a young dark-haired woman, stupidly pointing a long nosed single action revolver his direction—not to mention the two little girls. He took a step to the side to stand in front of the older girl and swung the little one by one arm to the ground with a backward push toward her sister.

He put his palms up. "I'm unarmed, mam. Not here to hurt anyone. I just needed to rest my horse. I slept in your barn last night."

The hammer was not cocked and her finger wasn't even close to the trigger. She was holding the grip with both hands, clearly as scared of the gun as she was of him. As unsteady as she was, this was an accident waiting to happen.

He walked toward her as quickly as he dared and closed a hand over the barrel and cylinder. "Let go of the gun before somebody gets hurt. It's clear that you don't know how to use it."

She held on and stared him in the eyes, trying to size up the moment. He was right. She had never held a gun in her hands before this minute. She wanted to let it go—She wanted to unlock her eyes from his big brown-eyed gaze, but she couldn't seem to do either. She wasn't afraid of him. He seemed kind and sincere enough. But she was still reeling from the shock of hearing her baby's screams out in the near darkness when she should have still been asleep in her bed. Then, seeing her in the arms of a strange man. No one ever came up here. Why was he here on this mountain?

"It's okay, mam. You and your girls are safe with me. I'm Andy Parker. I took the liberty of using your barn to rest here last night. I'll pay you for your trouble and be on my way." He wondered where her husband was. He couldn't help but notice how beautiful she was. Thick wavy dark brown hair hung down her back in a wild, silky mess. In fact, both girls had identical hair, just like their mama.

She suddenly let go of the gun when both girls ran to her, wrapping their arms around her.

"Mama, I hungry now." Rachel's squeaky little voice whined.

"Me, too. Want us to go look for eggs?" Emma Jo offered.

Andy glanced at both girls, then indirectly back at the woman while he checked the gun cylinder. It was empty.

"Yes, please. Look for eggs." She knew there probably wouldn't be any yet, if today at all. *Please let there be eggs, God.*

The pair took off for a small chicken coop that was built against the side of the barn. As Andy watched them go, he spied the jersey cow in an outdoor run just off the far end of the barn.

He looked back at the woman who seemed to be doing some heavy thinking.

"Mam?" He held out the gun, the grip toward her.

She slowly reached out and took it, letting her arm hang down, pointing the barrel at the ground. She raised her face to look him in the eye and reached out her hand. "I'm Summer Logan."

Andy quickly took her hand—the thick callouses on her palm not escaping his notice.

"My pleasure, Summer."

"What are you doing up this way, Andy?"

The way she said his name made him feel almost like an old friend. "Well, I'm not real sure. I was driving through a place called Forest Valley and somehow got off on the wrong road. My horse needed a rest and I came up on your place. I'm sorry I put a scare into everyone."

"Joe said there wasn't anything up the mountain for a long way. I've never been any farther than here."

He glanced toward the house and she knew he was wondering about Joe. "My husband died last year."

"So, it's just you and these two girls?"

"Yes."

He motioned toward the old pickup. "Does the truck run—get you to town and back for groceries and things?"

She shot a quick glance at it, then back at him, hesitated before nodding her head.

A slight smile pulled his lips. "Or...maybe not?" It was obvious the truck hadn't been moved in a long time.

Both turned at the sound of the girls running back.

"Mama, there's no eggs."

"No egg."

"It's just too early in the morning. I'll get Billie milked and get us…" She turned and headed for the barn without finishing what she was saying.

Little Rachel clung to Emma Jo's arm and both looked up at Andy.

"Mama makes biscuits for our food and eggs," declared Emma Jo, "but we don't have any eggs so we have to drink milk now cause the flour is gone."

Andy knew exactly what she was telling him, being well used to hearing little one's talk, listening to his brother and sister and cousin on the ranch, plus all the *baby* dudes who visited the ranch with their families every year.

"Well, girls, you want to help me feed my horse?"

"Yeah!" squealed Emma Jo while Rachel clapped her hands and giggled.

They ran on ahead of Andy, his main priority at the moment, to find out how much milk this Billie gave and check out Emma's declaration that they didn't have any food left.

He took his time letting them each toss some hay down for Sugar Beet while he brought in a scoop of grain from the dually.

"Emma Jo, can you show me where to get water?"

"In the kitchen. Come on." She ran out and toward the back of the house, Rachel on her heels.

He followed them inside through the open screen door. A pump handle as old as the house brought water from pipes poking through the wall at the sink. He set his bucket down and primed the pump. To his amazement, cold clear spring water gushed out. It felt to Andy like he'd stepped back in time—*way* back!

After filling the bucket, he glanced around the small kitchen. *No way!* The cook stove was a wood burner. The kitchen table looked home made with benches along each side. The floor was next to gone—old pieces of plywood that had been nailed over holes was nearly rotted away. Despite all of that, he noticed how extremely clean the kitchen was.

He lifted the bucket of water out of the sink and turned to head out, but Summer had quietly entered the doorway—a stricken look on her face. He set the water down and saw that her milk bucket had no more than a half cup in it. She was fighting to not cry.

"I need to ask a favor of you, Mr. Parker." She spoke so low, her face toward the floor, he had to work to hear her.

"It's Andy, and I'll help you any way I can."

"Me and my babies need a lift into town, if you don't mind. I can pay you a little bit. We will be staying there for a while, so you don't have to bring us back."

"I'd be happy to take you ladies anywhere you want to go. Do you have family in Forest Valley?"

"Friends."

"Okay. What about Ms. Billie out there and the chickens?"

"I'll put out lots of hay and the chickens just run free and eat what they find anyway. I'll find somebody to get them—to take them for free."

He nodded, choosing not to make that a burden for her right now. The way he saw it, she had more than her fair share to deal with. He mentally noted to make sure those animals were taken care of before he left town.

"Ya'll go on and get dressed, girls." She glanced at Andy. "I'll get our stuff and we'll be out in a few minutes."

"Mama, I hungry." Rachel began to cry.

"Soon as we get to town, I'll get you something." Summer's heart was breaking.

"No, Mama. I hungry. Rachel picked up the milk bucket and turned it up to drink the little bit it held. Before anyone could grab it, she poured it out all at once, splattering her face and gown. She began to wail at her predicament.

Andy grabbed a towel off the cabinet and squatted down in front of her. He wiped her face and arms, but he knew her continued crying was hunger pains.

"Rachel, I've got some food in my truck."

Immediately he had her attention, along with Emma Jo's.

"I hab it?" Rachel whined.

"Absolutely you can have it. As soon as you get dressed and ready to go to town, you and sister can eat in the truck. Hurry up now."

Both girls ran to another part of the house. Summer Logan stood staring in awe at Andy, just realizing that God must have heard her prayers and provided food for her kids on the first day that she couldn't feed them. HE must have sent this man.

Andy stood and patted her upper arm. "You better get ready to go. I'll hay and water your cow and get my horse loaded."

Nodding, she left the kitchen.

Andy parked his rig, with the Logan ladies aboard, in front of the Forest Valley Feed and Seed as Summer instructed and cut the engine.

She jumped out. "I'll be right back."

He watched her step up onto the front-loading dock and disappear inside.

Her first goal was to find a job. She was strong physically and hoped Wilbur Canton would let her work for him. Then she could look for somewhere to live. Maybe make a trade with Billie and the chickens for a month's rent. She'd get it figured out. At least she had the kids in town where she could get food and other things they needed.

"Well, well…look who's back in town?"

Summer turned toward the back corner where bags of feed were stacked high against the wall. She knew the voice, but it took a few seconds to locate him. Finally, he stepped out in the open.

"Hello, Mr. Canton."

"I thought you was long gone from here. What can I do for you?" He glanced out of the open store front. "You come in that rig out there?" He squinted at her as if he didn't like that idea.

"Yes, he gave me and the girls a ride. I wondered if you might have a job here at the store for me. I'm strong. I can work hard."

He sized her up and down before answering. "Where you living at?"

"I've got to find a place. I just got to town."

"Thought you was going off to live with your folks."

"Well...I...that didn't work out."

"My apartment upstairs is still available."

"But...you live there and I don't..."

"I been staying in my back room down here. I don't climb the stairs too good anymore. You and them little girls can live up there."

It felt like a heavy weight just lifted off her shoulders. "Thank you. But I still need a job."

He nodded. "I could use some help. We'll see how you work out for me."

It suddenly felt like Christmas morning. "When do I start?"

"How bout you get settled in up there and we'll look at starting in a day or so. It's all furnished. You just need your personal effects."

"Thank you, Mr. Canton. I'll work hard."

She walked briskly out to the truck and opened the back door where the kids were strapped in seat belts. "Come on, girls. We've got a place to stay and I got a job so I can take care of us."

Once her girls and the single bag of stuff were out, she opened the front passenger door. "I can't thank you enough, Andy, for all your help. I know God Himself sent you up the mountain last night because I prayed every day for help."

She quickly explained the job and the upstairs apartment, pointing to the stairs on the outside of the building. "It's a new start for us."

Her excitement was genuine, almost like a kid with a new toy. But, Andy got an odd feeling as he watched the man peep out of the store entrance and stare hard at Summer's back while she was so excitedly talking to him. The expression on his face was one of disgust, his squinty eyes giving off something that made Andy's skin crawl.

"That's great, Summer. I'm glad I could help. So…is this man who hired you a friend of yours?"

"Actually, he owns this store. Joe worked for him sometimes when we needed money."

"I see. Well, guess you should arrange for Miss Billie's care and those dozen chickens."

"I'll ask Mr. Canton if he wants them."

At that, she steered the girls toward the end steps to the loading dock and hurried back inside.

Andy got out, unable to drive away and leave the trio there without knowing if they were in a safe place. He helped the little ones up the steps and herded them inside.

Summer was fully engaged in explaining her predicament with the animals until the store owner spotted him and rudely, physically pushed past her. He pasted on a toothy smile, but those eyes held on to their repugnance.

"Come in, sir. Can I help you today?"

Andy nodded toward Summer whose eyes spoke volumes for her feelings—rejection, unworthiness. It broke his heart, while he battled with the near overwhelming desire to put the man's lights out for him for the rest of the day!

"I can wait. I believe the lady was talking to you first." Andy's look and tone brought the middle aged, graying man up short just as he was about to wave her off as not important.

"Er…uh…she just sold me some livestock" He turned his head toward her. "We'll go up after them after closing, Ms. Logan."

Emma Jo and Rachel stood quietly beside Andy, holding hands. He wondered if they were feeling the oppressiveness in the room.

"Alright then, I guess we're all set." Summer had lost a little of her steam after Mr. Canton bumped her shoulder to get her out of his way. She walked up to Andy and offered her hand. He covered it with both of his over-sized ones and wished her well. Canton's whole body stiffened at Andy's style of a hand shake. He seemed to have just realized that he was the driver of the dually out front.

Squatting down to pint-size level, he pushed his straw Stetson off his forehead and rested his hands on each of the children's waists. "I'm really glad I got to meet you two. Emma Jo and Rachel, I'll always remember you. I gotta go now."

He stood up seconds before Emma Jo grabbed him around the legs and began to cry. "I don't want you to leave us. Tell him, Mama. You can stay with us."

"Stay wit us." Rachel cheeped, but didn't move from where she stood.

Summer was shocked at Emma Jo's reaction and rushed to pull her away. She took both girls by a hand and instructed them to tell Mr. Parker goodbye.

"No!" Emma Jo hid her face in her mother's jean clad leg.

"They'll be fine, Andy. Just go. Thank you again for everything."

The glance he shot her before turning and walking out, grabbed Summer's heart string until a huge lump threatened. What did she just see in those huge, kind eyes?

***

CHAPTER FOUR

There had been a few tough situations that Andy had endured during his life, but driving out of Forest Valley, knowing he would never see the three Logan girls again or know if they were all right—or hungry—or being abused by someone was overwhelming. He felt a heart sickness that he'd never felt before. He couldn't define it. It wasn't guilt like he'd felt when Reeny's baby died up in the cave years ago. Or grief over the loss of a loved one. Or fear when he'd had a psycho man holding a gun to his head in the dude ranch barn where he was hiding from the law.

After driving over a couple of hours, he stopped at a roadside park and unloaded Sugar Beet to rest and graze.

If the intensity of this *feeling*, whatever it was, didn't let up, he knew he would be throwing up the coffee and donut he'd swallowed before he left Forest Valley.

Maybe he was just still mad at that Canton fellow for the way he treated Summer. He'd felt anger at other people's words and actions before. Lots of times, in fact. But he couldn't recall ever *really* wanting to hit somebody—until today. Maybe that was it. He should have decked the sorry scoundrel. He should have demanded to see the apartment where they would be living. He should have gone after Miss Billie and the chickens himself to make sure they wouldn't be left to die slowly. He should have helped Summer move all the things she might have wanted to take—not leave her with nothing except a few raggy clothes and at the mercy of—*who.* His mind was racing faster than he could emotionally keep up.

He didn't really want to be so involved with that woman— didn't need the responsibility. His life was free and easy, just him and Sugar Beet. It had been almost four months since he'd left Wyoming and he was loving this carefree lifestyle. So, what was wrong with him suddenly.

"Oh, Jesus." He moved off the picnic table where he sat and went straight to his knees. He grabbed his hat by the brim and dropped it on the ground in front of him. He was fully aware that this break down he was experiencing was a spiritual thing—not just emotional and physical.

"Father, what's the matter with me? What do You want from me? It seemed so right when I left home to travel. You have blessed me all these months, at every rodeo and on the road. I know it was You who sent me up that mountain to rescue that little family. What am I missing?" he cried out. *"What am I not doing that you've taken Your Peace from me?"*

He had no idea how long he was waiting, agonizing in prayer, but he did know His Lord's Voice when He finally spoke—

I SEEK NOT MINE OWN WILL, BUT THE WILL OF THE FATHER WHICH HATH SENT ME.

As those Words abruptly filled his mind, a knowing of what he had done, where he had messed up, settled fully in his spirit. Andy raised up straight on his knees, eyes wide. Shame filtered through him then as he understood what he was being told. He knew with no doubt nor hesitation what his Father was saying.

Forgive me, Lord. I'm so sorry. I guess I just got carried away. Father… I choose again right now…not my will, but Your Will. Just Yours.

He jerked his head up, realizing Sugar Beet was loose and he didn't know how long he'd been praying. But, the pony hadn't moved from the spot beside the trailer where he was ankle deep in rich, green grass.

Within ten minutes he was loaded and back on the road, headed for Forest Valley, Idaho.

So—he knew the basic thing he needed to do, which was to go back and complete his mission of helping Summer Logan and her children. He hadn't done everything he was sent there to do. What he didn't know was exactly what that *everything* amounted to.

There was an excitement stirring inside him now. Partly because he already missed those two little ladies who were crying because he had to leave and partly because his spirit was soaring with the energy of the Holy Spirit—knowing he was moving the right way with his Father. God had practically had to grab him by the scruff of his neck and yank a time or two to make him recognize that he'd taken a wrong turn. The next step would have been the old Heavenly wood shed. He had to smile at that thought. He *did not* want to go that far with God. He'd been there—done that! A quick, sharp turn to the Right was far better.

Andy believed his Heavenly Father had given him the past months to fulfill a dream of hauling down the rodeo road, but he wasn't listening to know when he was being called away from that to a special mission. His own way and desires had jumped in the driver's seat.

Now, he was focused exclusively on whatever he was led to do when he got back to the girls.

Summer took the girls up the stairs located on the outside of the store along the end wall.

The first thing the three of them noticed as soon as they stepped inside was the awful stench. Trash littered the floor, table, counter top and stove top in the one-room apartment.

All three grabbed their noses and moaned. Summer could see that the mattress on the one full sized bed was so black nasty, it wasn't fit for man or animals. In all her young life, living homeless, she'd never seen anything this sickening. She backed out the doorway. Both kids had already turned and run halfway back down the stairs.

"Don't either of you say a word about that smell. Let *me* do the talking." She looked straight at Emma Jo.

"Okay."

"K."

Back inside the store, Mr. Canton frowned when he saw them. "Should be about nap time for them two, ain't it?"

"Well, um, we were thinking we really need a few more things from our cabin. I suppose, if you don't mind, we can go on up and get the cow and chickens, and we could pack the things we forgot. I'm sure you wouldn't want anything to happen to the animals, being as they belong to you now."

He stared at her, not liking a woman who did too much thinking or tried to call the shots for him. But, he figured on going up after the animals anyway. He'd make sure she learned her place soon enough.

"Yeah, I believe now is as good a time as any while business is slow. I'll get my truck and stock trailer and a few cages for the birds."

"Mama, can we stay at our house? I don't like it here." Emma Jo pulled on Summer's shirt, her little voice and eyes begging.

Before she could answer, Wilbur Canton wheeled around and pointed his fat finger at her face. "Your house is upstairs now, little girl, and you and your sister better be getting on up there and stay put until me and your mama get back here with that cow."

His angry bark sent both girls running behind Summer and grabbing both her legs, their faces stuck to the cheeks of her rear end.

It took a few seconds to absorb what Mr. Canton had just said to her children—and the way he'd said it. Not in this lifetime would her babies spend one second in that disease infested hole up there. She couldn't allow them to get stranded again up on the mountain either with no way to get food. She needed this job—but a clean place to sleep.

A plan had formed in her mind coming down the apartment stairs a few minutes ago and she could still get that done, but her girls staying alone—No!

"They're too young to stay alone, Mr. Canton. They go where I go."

Scowling at her now, she could see him struggling to hold his temper in check.

"Well...I believe they need to be sitting in car seats according to the law. I can't chance getting a ticket for that." He scratched his head and stared a few seconds into space. "I'll be right back," he mumbled, as he brushed past her and left.

She pushed a sudden rush of nausea down with a couple of ragged breaths and worked hard to think clearly. Apparently, she had made a terrible mistake getting mixed up with this man, but she needed her quilts and the one sleeping bag that belonged to Joe from the house.

"Them girls will stay across the street with a family member of mine. She agreed to watch them long enough for us to get there and back," Canton growled as he stomped back inside. He jerked his arm toward the door. "Ya'll get on over to that cafe there and sit down in there and be quiet til we come get you."

"Mama, we want to stay with you." Emma Jo began to cry loudly, then Rachel joined in.

"That's enough from both of you," Canton stepped threateningly towards them.

"Mr. Canton," Summer swallowed hard to quell the blast of words sitting on her tongue, "these are *my* children. I can take care of them."

His mouth shut and tightened in anger.

She put her arms around them in a tight hug. "Hush now. We'll be just fine."

Without looking at him, she softly asked, "What's this family member's name?"

"Juda Waller. She's my sister. She'll feed them while we're gone."

"Well, girls, lets walk across the street and meet Ms. Juda Waller. Let's go see what good things she has to eat."

Once outside, she sucked a deep, all the way to her soul, breath. It took every ounce of restraint she had to calm herself, as she slowly walked with the kids to the cafe. *Think, Summer!!*

An extremely overweight woman sat at a table that seemed to serve as the check out just inside the cafe door. Cigarette smoke created a hazy sadness throughout the small cave-like room. A couple of men occupied a center table—drinking coffee and smoking. Neither looked up when Summer and the girls entered, but a big smile greeted them from the woman by the door.

"Well these must be my wards for a couple hours."

"Juda Waller?"

"That would be me. And you?"

"I'm Summer Logan. This is Emma Jo and Rachel. They won't be any trouble and I won't be gone any longer than necessary."

Summer knelt down between them. "Girls, you mind Ms. Waller and stay out of the way. I'll be back as quick as lightening."

Both girls looked like they were about to cry.

"Now if you kids would go sit at that table there, I'll order you some hamburgers." Juda's constant smile and gentle voice was barely enough encouragement for Summer to leave them there.

The pair walked hand in hand to the table pointed out to them and Summer went out the door quickly before she changed her mind. Nothing felt right about this—the job—the trip to her cabin with Mr. Canton—But she had asked for it herself. She just had to work her way through it.

Jesus, help me and my girls find our way. Thank You.

Andy parked in front of the feed store around mid-afternoon. A young cowgirl was pushing and pulling on the double doors, then cupped her hands around her eyes trying to see inside through a small glass pane.

"Dang it," she exploded, just as Andy stepped out of his dually.

"Is it locked up?" he asked, as his eyes darted around the area.

"Yes, and the stupid sign says it's open. Good luck getting anything out of here." She let loose with a string of her impatience and got in her pickup and left.

Andy tried the doors. Locked tight. Lights inside were off. He went around to the apartment stairway that Summer had pointed out that morning and went up. He knocked loud enough to wake the dead, but no answer. The door was unlocked, so he cracked it open. Before he could open his mouth to yell inside, the putrid smell made him jerk back. He shoved the door all the way open then and stepped inside. The stink and filth he saw was unbelievable and thankfully there was no sign of the girls having been there. He shut the door behind him and raced back to his rig.

The only thing he could think of was maybe they had all gone up to Summer's cabin to get the livestock.

He sat behind the wheel, thinking. He knew for a fact Summer wouldn't be staying in that apartment. Maybe she changed her mind and Mr. Canton took them back up the mountain to leave them there. His mind flashed the picture then of how rude Canton had been to Summer earlier that day. It was a long way up there. How could he be sure that's where they were?

Then he recalled seeing an old white paint-peeled stock trailer parked up against the other side of the store. He jumped out and raced to look. It was gone.

His heart was pounding. Something felt all wrong here. He knew he had to head up to the old cabin. He pulled back onto the road and went a block down to where the mountain road began. A quick glance in his side view mirror turned into a double-take and a moment of pure unbelief. He stopped dead in the center of his turn. "My sweet Holy Jesus!"

Little Rachel was running behind his trailer in the middle of the road, screaming and crying. "Anny. Anny."

He jumped out and in five strides, scooped her up in his arms. She was screaming hysterically. "I've got you, Rachel. You're safe, baby girl. I've got you." He looked around, but there wasn't another soul on this little back street. Not even Emma Jo.

Back inside the truck, he backed his trailer and headed back around to the feed store. Rachel still had his neck firmly in her grasp. He kept one arm tight around her to settle her down, hoping she could show him where her sister was.

"Rachel, listen now. Can you show me where Emma Jo is so we can go get her?" Her crying had simmered to a series of hiccups.

"Mama gone."

"Where's Mama?"

"Mama gone."

"Rachel, where is Emma Jo?"

She raised up and looked out the passenger window, then pointed across the street.

He climbed out with Rachel clinging to him by both arms and legs. He carried her across the street and forcefully untangled her from around him to stand her on the sidewalk, then squatted to her level.

"Hold my hand, Rachel, and take me to where Emma is."

She pulled him to the cafe door and when he entered, Juda's face lit up like a beacon from her chair by the door.

"Well, come on in cowboy!"

When she spied Rachel, her face lost the smile. "I see you found my little runaway. I appreciate you bringing her back. Now *you* get over there at that table and stay put while I wait on this nice young man."

Andy picked her back up, ignoring the woman, and demanded, "Where is Emma Jo?"

"I don't know who you think you are, Mister, but…"

Rachel pointed toward a swinging door and Andy immediately pushed through it.

"Hey, you can't go in there. That's private."

A grey haired elderly woman was laboring over the stove without looking up and Emma Jo stood on a bucket trying to wash dishes. There were at least a week's worth of dirty dishes and pots, on a good business week, stacked everywhere. Emma Jo didn't turn around when they entered the kitchen.

He put Rachel down.

"Emma Jo?" Andy called softly to her.

When she turned her face toward Andy, he was suddenly torn by rage and a cracking heart. She was soaking wet and her eyes were swollen from crying

She dropped the plate into the water and stepped down from the stool. Slowly she walked to him, then stood staring at the floor. Her face crinkled and tears poured when he picked her up and held her. Rachel had him around the leg, quietly staring up at her sister.

Andy grasped Rachel's hand and left the cafe without a word to the woman—Just left her glaring.

Emma Jo sat in his lap in the truck while Rachel perched on top of his center console box.

"Emma Jo, did anybody do anything to you…to hurt you?"

"No. But Ms. Waller said my mama wasn't coming back until I washed all the dishes cause I had to pay for our food we ate."

He took both of her tiny hands in his big ones and turned them over, then back. "How long were you in there washing those dishes?"

"I washed ten whole plates and I think a hundred forks.

Andy nodded in all seriousness. "Well, I believe she has been well paid for her food. What do you think?"

"Well, we only got a half of a hamburger each. *I* think I have some change coming."

Andy laughed out loud. This five-year-old is headed for the White House someday, he'd bet on it. He was relieved on one hand, but the other hand wanted to make a fist and pound it into somebody's face.

"Do you know where Mama went, Emma?"

She looked up at him, seemingly in thought. "My name is Emma Jo, but *you* can just say Emma if you want to."

He smiled. This little girl sure knew how to make a fella feel special. "Thank you."

"Mama went to get Billie and our chickens."

"Okay. I think we'll just head up there and see if she needs our help. You two get in the back seat and I'll fix your seat belts."

"Okay."

"K"

Andy drove as safely as he could, but still hurry. By the time he reached the cabin, Canton's stock trailer was backed into the barn. Both girls were sound asleep and he hoped they would stay that way until he checked out this situation.

He parked at the entrance of the driveway and shut off the motor. He got out, locking the girls in and walked quietly to the barn.

At first, it was only silence. Then like a bomb that suddenly detonated— "I swear, I'll run this through your guts if you move, Wilbur Canton."

"Girl, I can wait you out all night if I have to. Nobody's going to help you out here. You just need to be taught a real good lesson in where a woman's place is. And it ain't smart-mouthing a man who's doing you favors."

"I don't want your favors."

"You got nobody but me, girl."

Andy knew he had a clear shot if it came to that, but he doubted that would happen. This man was no more than a thieving coward and probably worse than that if he thought he could get by with it. At least the trailer wasn't loaded yet. He just needed to get this over with right now.

He grasped his 9mm that he'd pulled from his locked glove box and stuck in his back-waist band. Grandpa Hank had taught him how to carry and use this pistol with a lot of practice through the years, but this was the first time he was faced with the real deal. He cocked it at the same instance he stepped inside where he could be seen.

"Now, that's not quite true, Mr. Canton. Ms. Logan has God, a whole host of angels, me and a 9mm…all staring at your fat head. She's got favor all around her and I believe *she said*— correct me if I'm wrong—she does *not* want *your* favors. It's time for you to leave."

The shock of Andy's sudden appearance rendered both Summer and Canton speechless. She let down her guard just long enough to allow Canton to lunge for her, but she was as quick as a lightning bolt. She brought the pitchfork in her hands down with the strength of a man and buried the prongs perfectly over each of his wrists where they grabbed for her ankles. He was pinned to the ground, unable to break the hold.

Andy returned the hand gun to his back waistband as he quickly went to Summer and pulled her away from her captured prey and to the barn doorway.

"Keep your eye on him. If his hands get loose, yell and run out of here. I'll take care of him. I need to make sure he doesn't have a firearm in his truck."

She didn't respond, even though she heard and was prepared to do what he said.

"Summer!" He grasped her upper arm and jostled her to attention. "Watch him."

She nodded up and down rapidly. "I will. I am." The turn of events in the past five minutes had her in a mild shock. She stared at Canton's hands held together by her pitchfork prongs. She had no clue how she did that. Acting through an adrenaline rush was one thing, but this almost felt like someone else had control of the fork.

Andy finished searching the truck inside and underneath, then the stock trailer. Satisfied Canton wasn't armed, he opened his driver side door and went further inside to release the man so he could get out of here before Andy lost it on him.

He trained his shooter on him again, then easily lifted the fork off his wrists. "Canton, you've got twenty seconds flat to get in that pickup and drive out. Don't make the mistake of showing back up here."

In less than a minute, his tail lights shown on the road. Andy followed him out on foot until his rig disappeared over a hill.

He walked past his dually and peeped through the glass. The kids were still sacked out. Good—because from the look he'd seen on Summer, he still had something to deal with there.

He replaced his gun once again in his waistband as he slowly approached her. She hadn't moved a muscle.

"Summer?"

She raised her eyes up to his, didn't say a word, but her eyes pooled and spilled over.

Slowly he reached both arms out and wrapped her up in a tight hug. He felt her body trembling hard. She was crying, not making more than a tiny mewling sound.

All at once, she pulled loose from his grip. "Andy, my babies are in town. We have to hurry. I…Oh, God…I left them with strangers. It wasn't a good place." She pushed him away and ran toward the dually.

"Wait a minute." He caught her arm.

"No! I can't wait."

"Summer, look right here."

He showed her where to look through the dark tinted windows into the back seat.

When she spied her girls sleeping in Andy's back seat, she lost all the fight she had in her and collapsed to sit on the ground beside the truck. Leaning against the step side, she dropped her head down and cried in a way she hadn't allowed herself to do since Joe died.

He gathered her up and so gently lifted her into his arms. This girl couldn't weigh a hundred pounds all wet!

She didn't argue, but relaxed against his chest and buried her face in his jacket. It was just dawning on him that neither she, nor the girls had coats on. It would be dark and getting colder in a couple hours.

A glance down at her face grabbed his heart. She was still crying, but so silently. The emotional battle was all over her face as she strained to not make a sound—tears were pouring.

He carried her inside through the back door and quickly found her bedroom. He laid her on the soft quilt covering the bed and covered her with a second one he found folded on top of an old trunk.

He bent close and whispered in her ear, "You need sleep, sweet girl. I'll take care of your little ones."

There was no response and she had stopped crying. She was already asleep.

SURRENDERED VI

He wondered if she'd had a bite to eat all day. Luckily, he had restocked his cooler after leaving Forest Valley this morning—bread, ham, cheese and a half gallon of orange juice. Thank God, he could at least feed them until he could get to a grocery store for staples.

He stopped when he realized what he'd just said. *Yes...Thank God!! And I do thank you, Lord Jesus, for all your help—for helping Summer pitchfork that dude to the ground. That was a good one! And for seeing that I didn't wind up back out here without any food, and especially thank You for letting Rachel recognize my rig and chase after me. Thank you for — everything!*

"Andy! Andy!"

Emma Jo's voice rang out from the back of the house.

"Look! Eggs!" She held up a plastic bucket.

He rushed outside to see a grin spread across her entire face. Joy like he was seeing on her can't be bought.

"Hey, that's awesome, Emma. How many did you get."

"Six. Rachel is still asleep."

"Your mama is asleep, too."

"I know. I saw you carry her in the house."

He smiled and took the bucket from her. "I'll set this in the kitchen, then you and I need to go put Sugar Beet in a pen and feed him."

She clapped her hands with pure joy. "Oh—I'm so happy. Come on, lets hurry. That horse is very hungry."

He laughed. "How do you know?"

"Be–cause, silly, he stomped his feet in the trailer and woke me up."

"Ah—well, that's a sure nuff sign alright."

That child's joy was contagious. Andy couldn't believe how happy *he* was feeling right now—and right in the middle of all this mess. Maybe, he decided, realizing he could still feel the pressure of Summer's trembling body against his broad chest, maybe it was the three beautiful, dark-haired messes he was now looking after. Their well-being was his responsibility for the time being—He just didn't know what he was going to do with them.

***

CHAPTER FIVE

The storm Andy had no idea was about to roll in—rolled in. And from the sound of it, it had no intention of taking any prisoners.

He was rolled up in his sleeping bag in the hay barn when the double doors blew open just a few feet from where he lay. The wind came over the barn, sounding like a full throttle freight train.

Just a couple hours earlier, he fed the girls ham sandwiches from his cooler, played hide and seek and gave piggyback rides until minutes before dark. He said prayers with them and tucked them into their beds just as darkness fell. Summer was still asleep when he headed for the barn.

Shortly after he laid down, two kicks and he was free of the insulated bag and back on his feet. He spoke to Sugar Beet as calmly as he could, hearing the pony's excitement in the pitch darkness. Debris of some kind rammed into the barn doors before flying on past. Then, more swirled and sailed inside the barn.

Andy dove into the hay, jerked a bale out of the stack and scrunched behind it.

"*Lord Jesus, let your angels protect the girls inside that house,*" he shouted.

Just as suddenly as the wind had come, it stopped. Rain began to pour along with the largest hail balls Andy had ever seen. They bounced inside the open barn doors and one landed on the hay bale he was crouched behind. He covered his head with his hands and imaged a picture in his mind of very large angelic beings covering each of the three girls. The pounding continued for several minutes before the storm lost its steam and quit.

He jumped up. The barn appeared to be intact. Racing outside, he blinked several times trying to see through the darkness. He got to the truck and pulled on the headlights.

The whole right side of the house was caved in or gone—the side where the bedrooms were.

He ran into the hole that used to be Summer's bedroom wall.

"Summer!"

"Here."

The sound was muffled, but he heard. He needed more light. He got back out to the truck, backed it up and headed the bright lights directly into the defaced bedroom. There were no longer separate bedrooms, but all opened into one mound of wet rubble.

"Summer! Emma Jo! Rachel! —Talk to me so I can find you." He prayed he'd hear a lot of chattering at once. He didn't know for sure who made the muffled sound a minute ago.

"Here."

"I hear you, Summer. I've got to lift some boards up. Hang on."

In a couple of minutes, he saw her blue print shirt. He lifted large pieces of plaster up and finally uncovered her. But not just her. Beneath her lay both girls curled up in little balls.

"Summer, are you hurt? Do you hurt somewhere?"

"No, I'm all right."

He grasped her around her slight waist with both hands and gently lifted her up. Emma and Rachel both popped up at once, seeming to be no worse for the wear. For once, Emma Jo didn't say a word.

"Girls, stand still until I get your mom outside. Then I'll come carry you over these boards." Both nodded vigorously, the only move made was Rachel reaching for Emma's hand.

Once everyone was out, they sat inside the warm truck.

"Ladies, we dodged a bullet tonight. A house fell in on all of you and nobody got a scratch that I can see. That's a miracle." Andy was surprised that he didn't have at least one hysterical female on his hands. Everybody was calm and quiet.

"Where did those people go?" Emma asked rather matter-of-factly.

Andy and Summer turned to look at her in the back seat.

"What people, Emma?" Andy asked, searching her face for signs of shock.

"Those ones who came with Mama to our room when the house fell down."

Summer's mouth fell open. "You saw them?"

Emma nodded. "Uh huh. They made light come so Mama could lay on top of us real fast."

Andy suddenly wanted to jump out and dance. He knew. The angels came to protect them.

"Did *you* see them?" He looked excitedly at Summer.

Her hand was covering her mouth to stifle the laughter that was bubbling up. "Oh, Andy! There were two of them. They woke me up and it felt like they carried me, sort of, to where the girls were. I heard all this noise, but I didn't feel anything except the girls curled underneath me."

Then, for the first time, it dawned on him that the girls were all three-bone dry. The rain had not wet any of them.

Andy had witnessed God's presence, His help and miracles all his life, but he never failed to be amazed and completely in awe every time he encountered his Father like this.

He and Summer sat silently for a bit with their own awe and thoughts about what had just occurred.

In a few minutes, he glanced over his shoulder at Rachel. She was already sound asleep, along with Emma Jo. When he glanced back at Summer, she was gazing thoughtfully at his face. He smiled at her and reached out and grasped her hand. Her fingers closed over his. The shudder that rippled through his body when she did that, caught him off guard. Her hand jerked slightly—Did she feel something, too? They both tightened their hold while their eyes locked in a warm admiration.

"I thought for a while that *you* were an angel," Summer whispered, without breaking eye contact. I was sure you would just evaporate after getting us to town. Why did you come back?"

He smiled, continuing to study the depths of those mahogany pools. "I guess two reasons. One is because I was worried about you and these girls. A couple hours up the road, I was already missing you. And two, God didn't want to hear my whining, so He told me to go back."

The smile that she graced him with was spread across the most beautiful face he'd ever seen in his life. He covered her hand with both of his, then reached and smoothed a hand over the front of her hair to push it back from her face—Dark eyes, and dark brown, long, jumbled up beautiful hair.

He wondered about that jolt he'd felt when he first touched her hand. He had never experienced such a thing before. Not with any girl he'd dated. Not even with Abby.

"I'm glad you came back. I missed you, too, Andy Parker."

He was amazed at that. She hadn't given him any indication that she thought anything about him, except grateful for helping her out of a tough spot. But then, he hadn't felt much about her either—not until this moment. He had thought she was pretty when he first saw her—even with her shooter aimed at his middle. He had been anxious over what condition he'd driven off and left her and the girls in. But this was a whole other perception.

He saw Summer as one who took things at face value. What was—was. He'd never heard her complain about anything. She *seemed* to just roll with the punches. But, he figured there was a box full of junk she was stuffing down inside of her, hiding it away—junk that sooner or later, would overflow and come out.

He nodded and gave her hand an extra squeeze. He wanted to kiss her. *Really* wanted to kiss her. Instead he opted to not rush her or him. They all needed to try and sleep the rest of the night. Tomorrow would bring some new busy plans with it, guaranteed.

"Let's get some rest. I have a better idea than this truck, though. Get Rachel and follow me."

He carried Emma to the barn and stood her beside him while he spread out his heavy insulated sleeping bag. With Summer on the inside and both girls side by side, he pulled the opened excess over them and zipped it on the end and half way up the side.

After building a two-bale enclosure around them for insulation, he wrapped up in his heavy overcoat and stretched out on the hay on the kids' side of the bedroll. Within minutes, they were asleep.

Dawn was just breaking when Andy's eyes opened. Both children were still sleeping hard, but Summer was gone.

The woodsy scent of pine smoke reached his senses, bringing him fully awake and to his feet. He stretched until he was sure he was another few inches taller, then walked outside into the sweet mountain air.

His breath went out with a gasp at the sight of his truck and trailer. Slowly he walked out to look closer. His rig was hail-beat all to smithereens. The windshield was still in one piece, thankfully, but the rest of it was the sorriest looking thing he'd ever owned.

When he glanced to the left, the daybreak showed up the total destruction of Summer's cabin. He didn't think it was much to begin with, but these Logan ladies lived here. It was their home—their security.

Where was Summer? What was on fire? He raced to the back of what was left of the place. From the back, the house mostly appeared normal. He opened the screen door and stepped into the kitchen—the only room still intact.

Summer was cooking breakfast on the old wood burning stove as if nothing had happened.

"Hi! Breakfast is almost ready." She whipped her head around toward him, smiled, then went back to her business.

There was a platter of ham and toast she'd obviously gotten from his cooler, and all six eggs from Emma's egg hunt yesterday were fried. His jug of orange juice was sitting on the table.

Andy was stunned. This woman was cooking and going on about her business as if her house hadn't just blown down around her a few hours ago.

"Summer, what are you doing in here?"

She stopped and turned, looking at him like he was the crazy one. "Well, the kitchen is still standing and we do have to eat."

He looked at the ceiling, then through the caved-in remainder of the cabin. "It's still standing for the moment, but it could come down on your head any time." His tone matched the frustration on his face.

"Well, it hasn't come down yet," she countered saucily, "and breakfast is ready."

No sooner than that tart little exchange took place, a plaster wall and framework from the ceiling fell in the floor just on the other side of the table.

He reached her in two strides and grabbed her wrist, pulling her out the door with him. "Stay here. I'll get the food."

She held the screen door open while he filled his hands with the platter of food and jug of orange juice.

He knew he shouldn't feel angry at her. She was trying to take care of her family. But she could have gotten herself hurt or killed.

After they settled themselves in the hay, Andy got paper plates and plastic forks from his supplies in the truck.

The girls didn't stir, so they ate their own portions in silence.

He was still fighting his irritation, but when he glanced at her downcast face, he knew he'd hurt her feelings. He finished and as soon as she put her plate aside, he got up and pulled her up with him. Nodding toward outside, she followed him to the back side of his trailer.

"I'm sorry, Summer. I didn't mean to be so rude to you. Thinking what could have happened to you in there…scared me."

She stared at the ground. "I figured you were hungry. I just wanted to …"

He cupped her face with both hands and lifted until he saw the tears glistening. At that moment, he knew this woman was the one he wanted. Every desire to love, to cherish and honor, to protect was awakened in his heart and soul like had never been before.

"I know," he whispered. "Me, too." He leaned down and touched his lips to hers. When she leaned into him, he kissed her deep and tenderly. He wrapped his arms around her and held her tightly against him, stroking her hair, letting her feel the security and protectiveness he offered.

Summer was surprised at the emotions this cowboy had awakened in her. She was just realizing how closed her heart had become since her husband died. The pain of losing Joe had been unbearable. She didn't believe she could ever feel love again for another man. But, remembering him now didn't evoke the pain she'd lived with for so long. Somehow it seemed that Joe was smiling, giving his blessing to her to move on, to be happy. In fact, she was sure of it.

She wrapped her arms tightly around Andy, feeling the tight muscles across his broad back. She wanted him to love and hold during long dark nights—to cook for and to make a real family with for her girls. She didn't even know him and yet, it felt like she'd known him for a long time. So strange.

Abruptly, the moment changed to panic when they both turned at the sound of crackling and popping of wood burning. Flames shot upward from the back of the house.

They ran in the direction of the barn, finding the girls still asleep. Within seconds, the old cabin was fully engulfed. The kitchen was dry and burned hot and fast. Thankfully, the past evenings rain had kept the fire from spreading past the house.

Andy stood beside Summer and watched everything she owned turn to ashes. She wasn't reacting—just solemnly staring with her arms wrapped around her middle. He didn't try to console her, but let her adjust privately to what was happening.

He felt them then, rather than saw them. When he turned toward the barn, the girls were standing as still and solemn as their mama, holding hands and watching the only home they'd ever known burn to the ground.

The heat from the blaze was now too hot to stand this close. He reached for Summer and caught her upper arm, forcing her several steps backward. Still, she stared ahead, almost transfixed by the dissolution of her home that was happening in front of her.

Andy stepped to the girls and squatted down in front of them. "Emma, Rachel, everything's going to be all right. I'm going to take care of both of you and your mom." Two sets of eyes turned to look into his. He could see Emma swallowing and fighting desperately to not let tears fall. "Emma, it's okay if you cry. I cry sometimes, too."

Without a word, she stepped into his arms and clung tightly around his neck. Her sobs were breaking his heart as he tightened his hold around her tiny little body.

Rachel went to her mom for comfort. She picked her up and carried her back inside the barn.

Andy followed her, still holding Emma tightly.

Once they were settled down enough, the girls ate heartily while Andy and Summer took care of Sugar Beet and Billie. There was very little conversation as each tried to assimilate their thoughts and come up with the next move to be made.

Andy knew immediately what he wanted to do. This little trio was his responsibility now, by God's own command, at least, to help them get settled somewhere safe. *He* wanted to load them up and take them back to High Point with him. But, he knew better than to assume any part of something that God had sent him to do.

Up to now, he had taken care of the Logan's as each moment presented itself. Now—a major decision had to be made that was not so in front of his face and instant.

He had to wonder if the intense feelings he had for Summer was something other than true, lasting love. Could a man fall in love—real love—this fast?

His Uncle Donny Brandon came to mind then. He had met and married Aunt Reeny in the space of only a week or so— And he had been sent by God to rescue her from a horrible situation. That was twelve years ago and those two still acted like silly newlyweds.

He watched her walk through the outdoor pen and open the gate so Billie could go out into a larger pasture. He swallowed hard at the sight of her. The idea of driving home and leaving her or the girls—anywhere, was crushing his heart. He wanted to hold her, kiss her, give her a new home with modern appliances and plenty of food. He wondered then where she had been raised, that she would settle for the hardships she had lived under out here. He knew nothing about her.

Summer lingered at the gate after twisting the baling wire around the post to hold the gate open.

She wasn't sure how it happened, but Andy Parker had settled heavily into her thoughts since the moment she saw him. Even though she hadn't trusted him at first, when she pointed Joe's old pistol at him, there was a gentle, peaceful look in his eyes and sound in his voice that seemed to draw her toward him. And the protective move he'd made when he put both of her babies behind him when she stupidly pointed the gun their way—that wasn't lost on her.

Of its own volition, her mind always filled itself with Joe, never giving her much rest from missing him. But Andy's face was the one she imaged now—the one whose arms she wanted to feel wrapped tight around her.

She turned around to find him leaning against the back of the barn, arms crossed over his chest, watching her in serious contemplation.

He had to be wondering how he was going to get out of this bind with her and two little girls. She had to stop dreaming and think—make some serious decisions, because right now, Andy was all the help she had. She needed to think up some sort of plan—now. Her family was certainly not his responsibility.

Every step she took back toward the barn was used trying to make that plan. She had never had a job, had nowhere to leave her babies, if she *did* find work. There wasn't one family member that she knew of to go to for help.

By the time she reached Andy, she attempted to walk past him into the barn. She was about to lose her fight with the tears stinging her eyes. She could *not* cry again. But his hand shot out and grasped her upper arm. He slowly pulled her back and around to face him.

He studied her face, recognizing the abuse she was putting her mind through. He had never seen a family of females, from the little ones to the oldest, refuse, with all their strength, to show emotion.

"Hey, young lady." He waited until she looked up at him. Without a thought, he put his hand on the top of her shoulder and rubbed his fingers on the side of her neck. "We need to figure out in what direction to head out of here today. Got any thoughts about that?" He opened the door for her to tell him where her family was.

Tears began to roll down her cheek as she swiped at them and fought hard to stop the flow. It wasn't working. "Oh no! I can't...cry. I can't." She tried to pull away, but his hold tightened.

"Why can't you cry? If I was you and just experienced everything you have in the past few hours—why, I'd be curled up in a fetal ball, bawling like a little baby."

"You don't understand about those things. Joe always said if we cry, then it means we're not having faith in God and He won't answer our prayers." She choked on a sob, trying to swallow it.

He gave her time to get better control of her emotions, but continued to lightly grasp the top of her shoulder.

"Summer, I want you to listen to me. I know Joe must have been a good husband to you and a good daddy to those sweet girls, but being good and kind doesn't mean we get everything right. Our understanding can get a little fuzzy about some things."

She was looking him in the eye, listening intently.

"God gave you those tears to use when you need them. It kind of lets some of the pressure off when life gets too hard." He squeezed her shoulder. "Like right now."

Her eyes filled again and she dropped her head to hide her face.

"Don't be ashamed of what God gave you, baby. It's all right to cry."

She leaned into him then and he wrapped her up and held her tight while she cried.

Tears dripped unashamedly off Andy's black-whiskered face into her hair, exposing the intensity of his feelings for her. He was glad she let it go, but the sound of her soul-deep pain was overwhelming.

An hour later, all four were loaded in the truck, mainly to get out of the chilly air.

"Summer, do you have any family that should be contacted? Parents? Siblings?"

She shook her head. "We went looking for my parents about a year after we were married. My mom had overdosed on drugs and died. My dad was in prison. We went there and tried to see him, but he refused to see me. Said for me to never come there again."

Andy sunk back into his seat and stared out the windshield. He didn't know what he had expected her to say, but it wasn't *that*. Had she *ever* had a life experience without this kind of hardship?

He gazed at her, trying to keep pity out of his eyes. "Did your parents have a home place or...anything that could...?"

"Andy," she cut him off and leveled a look at him that he hadn't seen on her before—A here's-the-deal, take charge kind of look. "I was raised in the back of a van. My dad only moved it when we were being noticed too much by the police or the child welfare people. I never went hungry. I had clothes, a warm coat and shoes and blankets that made a soft comfortable bed. My mama taught me to read and spell and do math. I had school workbooks in every subject. When I finished the ones she brought me, she would get more. She was very book-smart, but she and my dad took drugs. And I really don't think he was my dad. He's just all I ever knew. He didn't pay much attention to me."

The girls were giggling and playing a hand clap game in the back seat, thankfully oblivious to the conversation in the front seat.

Andy wasn't faring so well. There wasn't a cell in his brain that was prepared for the revelation Summer was laying on him.

Her look softened as she gazed into the space in front of her. "Then, Joe came up to the van one night when my parents were gone somewhere." She looked at Andy again. "I was seventeen. He was thirty. We were married soon after by the Justice of the Peace and he brought me here. I never had a home until this one."

Both were silent for a while until she looked up and found him staring at her as if he had never seen her before.

"I was happy here, Andy. Me and Joe and eventually, the babies."

She smiled suddenly and it looked like the sun had shot a beam of light across her face. "Joe taught me about Jesus. We read the Bible to each other and he taught me how to praise God. We would dance for Him sometimes." She paused and smiled faintly. "That all seems like such a long time ago now. All of it. Everything seems like... a lifetime ago."

He was staring at her as though she was talking in a strange language. "You don't know what I'm talking about, do you?" Her question came out more like a statement of fact.

"Actually...I completely understand you. I know Jesus, too. I was just thinking you might show me that praise dance sometime."

"Well, I could show you, but we always waited until dark and danced under the stars. I'm not sure it would be the same with..." She looked at the smoldering rubble and gestured toward it.

"I happen to believe there isn't a more perfect time than right here, right now. The Bible says we should praise God for *all* things—even the hard ones."

"I want to dance to Jesus." Emma Jo popped up over the console, her eyes alight with excitement.

"I dance…too."

Andy opened his door, jumped out and yelled, "Come on, girls, let's praise the Lord!"

Emma and Rachel climbed over the console and followed him out his open door. Their squeals and laughter was music to his soul.

Summer got out and catching the sudden excitement, she raised her arms high over her head and began to twirl slowly in place. "Like this," she instructed the others.

They all followed her lead and Andy began to pray aloud as they raised their arms and eyes toward Heaven. "Thank You, Jesus. We praise You today for everything."

The little girls jumped and twirled and shouted their thank you's.

After a minute, Andy and Summer stopped while the girls ran inside the barn still shouting and giggling.

Summer was quiet with a peaceful glow on her face.

Andy felt it, too. He stepped over and stood beside her.

"What am I going to do, Andy?"

After a prayerful few seconds, he said, "I have an idea."

She turned widened eyes on him, eager to hear his plan.

"My family lives near Jackson, Wyoming. We have a dude ranch a few miles out of town. I think you and those girls should go home with me and then you can take time to decide what you want to do from there."

Her eyes squinted in confusion. "Family?"

He couldn't help but smile. "My parents and young brother and sister—And grandparents and uncle and aunt."

"Does everybody live in one house?"

"No. The ranch is big enough for several houses. But we all share in the work and the fun. I promise, you'll love it and so will Emma and Rachel."

"But, where would me and the girls live? Whose house?"

"Well...we'll figure that out later. I might be able to get a small cabin just for the three of you. But the thing we know for sure is that you must go *somewhere*. Unless you have a better idea."

She shook her head back and forth while keeping those large brown, naive eyes glued to his. Her heart was going ninety to nothing, scarcely believing she was going to Andy's home.

"Then it's settled? You'll go with me?"

She slowly nodded, then whispered, "Okay."

***

CHAPTER SIX

Two days later at High Point Dude Ranch

Laura Brandon laid her hand on her chest and stared at her husband for a long minute. Finally, she recouped from the shock. "Oh, Jesse! Tell me again what he said—Every word!"

He grinned at his wife's incitement. That wasn't something he saw in her often. In fact, the last time was the morning Andy told her he was taking off to parts unknown. This time was because of his call to say he was on his way home.

"Take a deep breath, mama. No matter what this is about, it will work out. Always does."

"But—is the girl he's bringing home a *girlfriend?* Are they—?"

"I don't know, hon. He said she has two little girls and they're homeless. He wanted to rent one of the cabins for them and he'd explain more later."

"And they'll be here in two or three days?"

"That's what he said." Jesse chuckled.

By the faraway look she had on her face, she wasn't listening now, but planning, cleaning, making beds, cooking.

"There is only a couple of reservations left to fulfill for late season dudes," she reasoned aloud, "so Andy's guests should be able to choose the cabin they want. Let's see—I'll put them in the cabin in the little alcove. If she's afraid to be out of our sight, I'll change it to cabin number one so they can be closest to our back door. I better call Granny Martha and Hank. They'll be hurt if I don't let them know Andy's on his way home. I wonder if they've ever lived out in the country, or are they city—"

When she caught Jesse's risible expression from the corner of her eye, she stopped and looked fully at him. "What?" Her eyes rounded in pure innocence.

His grin broadened across his face as he reached for her and pulled her tightly up against him. She tilted her face upward, eager for his kiss. That was one thing her cowboy for the past eighteen years was never short of—deep kisses and tight hugs. The emotion in his eyes was the purest of love that filled her heart every day and every night and carried her through every good and bad day of their marriage—their life.

"I guess I was doing a lot of thinking out loud, huh?"

"You were killing the fatted calf, Mrs. Brandon. Our prodigal is coming home."

She laughed. "Well, how about you call Grandpa Hank over to cook it up for us. I've got a cabin to clean and beds to make."

"I'm on it."

But first, he laid another lingering kiss on her, followed by a wink that was full of promise—for later.

Her smile back at him spoke volumes and grew wider when she heard his growling moan as he went out the back door.

September was a busy month for the dude ranch. Cabins had to be deep cleaned and winterized, petting zoo pens walled in for extra warmth and a dozen other chores throughout the month in preparation for another cold Wyoming winter.

Andy had spent the past four months on the road with his roping horse, trying to rodeo away a broken heart. Apparently, he had *some* success—Today he was coming home, bringing a young homeless girl and her two small daughters with him.

Laura wasn't totally surprised at this. He had a reputation around home as a one-boy rescue squad—forever hauling a lost or injured *something* through the back door—rabbits, squirrels, a stray pup and even an orphaned fawn. Only one other time he brought home a person. A young man who had, for no reason, ridden a bus to Jackson Hole from Sacramento and stepped into the Burger Gettin Place to eat. Andy had explained later that the Holy Spirit told him to go there and when he saw the man sitting there, he *knew* he was to bring him home to High Point—Simple as that!

Beau Doss, who later discovered he was Beau Vance, became one of the best cowhands in the area and Andy's close friend for the past six years. He and his wife, Carly, lived and worked on the ranch, becoming as close to the Brandon's as family.

Laura couldn't help but wonder if Andy's new undertaking was Heaven sent or—something else. What she *did* know was that she could hardly wait for them to arrive. Whatever this was about, it would work out, as Jesse had said. Andy was only twenty-four years old—young in years, but that young body carried an old soul. He'd always tended to think more like an adult, even as a child. Oh, she knew he wasn't infallible—No one is. He was just more mature thinking than most his age.

The whole ranch had heard the news of Andy's soon arrival today. His last phone call gave his approximate time to arrive around 5 or 6pm. They were coming hungry and tired.

Donny and Reeny had helped Grandpa Hank with preparing food, while Granny Martha and Laura readied the cabin for the Logan family. A reception was planned for supper on the pavilion.

"Unca Beau! Unca Beau!" Little Donny left his dump truck in the sand pile behind the chuck wagon where his mom was wiping down the prep table and ran toward the approaching horse and rider.

Beau pulled up and quickly dismounted, then reached his arms out for the boy racing toward him. He scooped him up in a bear hug, loving the little pats on his back from Donny and Reeny's young boy. Donny Hank Brandon was coming up on four years old and had called him Uncle Beau since he could talk.

"Hey there, dude."

"I'm not dude!"

Beau feigned surprise with an open mouth and wide eyes. "You're not! Well, what are you, then?"

"Unca Beau, you know I a real cowboy."

"A real one, huh. So, how many steers did you rope today."

He held up five stubby fingers. "This many."

"How many is that?"

"Five…and a hundrert."

Beau chuckled. "Well, then, I'd say you sure are a real cowboy."

"Yep. I'm hungry."

He laughed again and set him on his feet. In seconds, he disappeared behind the chuck wagon.

"Hello, Beau," Laura greeted him as she walked past toward the pavilion carrying a smoking bowl of something.

Hey, Ms. Laura. Any word from Andy?" He hollered after her.

"They'll be here any minute." She stopped then and turned around. "You and Carly be ready for supper in the pavilion as soon as they get here."

"Yes, mam."

Beau had missed the camaraderie with Andy during the long work days, especially while working cattle on the Double OO. Andy was the first true friend he'd ever had and he'd had to work hard to keep a right perspective when Andy told him he was leaving the ranch indefinitely. He hadn't expected him to stay gone the entire summer, but truth was, he needed this time away from his buddy. He'd become dependent on him to the point that he'd feel panicked when he wasn't close by to help him out of a tight spot. That was probably because Beau had never ridden a horse or thrown a rope before coming to live at High Point. Strangely he'd taken to it like a duck to water, but he still needed to mature up emotionally in some ways.

Carly had helped him considerably since they married a few years ago. She was new to this cowboy lifestyle too and looked to Beau to teach her the ways of ranch life. He had to strut around like he knew all about it, always worried that she'd see through his lack of knowledge. If she did, she never let him know.

But, his real confidence had grown tremendously over the past months until he felt as though he'd finally come into his own place in life—become his own independent man. But, with that independence from needing to prop himself on another person, he'd quietly drawn closer and more dependent on his Heavenly Father. As contradictory as that sounded—it felt more and more right as time went on.

He turned to lead his horse into the barn when he saw Carly coming toward him. She had gone shopping for groceries and other household essentials in town this morning.

"Hi," she said, a smile stretching across her luscious pink lipstick mouth.

That smile was not unusual. His wife was one of the most joyful, smiley people he knew—Always greeting everyone, including the horses and dogs, with that happy face. But something more had arrested his attention. Was it her eyes twinkling extra bright and fast? Was her hair different? No, that silky white-blonde ponytail was swishing behind her head as usual.

"Hi, yourself." He put his arm around her and pulled her close against his side. "Come with me to put this tired girl in her stall and you can tell me about your shopping trip. And, by the way, Andy and his guests are due home any minute. We're having supper for them in the pavilion."

"Oh fun! I wondered what was going on with all the food out here."

He took his arm from around her and she stood back to let him enter the barn with his sweaty young *coworker*. While he carried the saddle and pad to the tack room, she picked up a brush that was left lying on the concrete floor near the stall and began a welcomed grooming, massaging the mare's itchy back with the soft bristles.

Five minutes later, Beau slid the stall door shut and pulled down the latch. Fresh water, a handful of grain and a flake of alfalfa hay finished the work day for Miss Belle.

He hung the halter and lead rope on a peg beside the stall door and turned to face his wife. Her smile was instant and genuine—but different. Maybe her make-up was different. She usually wore some when she went to town. With or without it, she was the most beautiful creature God ever made.

They stared at each other for a long, silent moment, both drinking in the other like newlyweds. He reached a finger up to push some stray wisps of hair away from her eye when she suddenly took on a more serious expression—a soft, sweet, peaceful look that clearly said she had something particular to say.

"I…did more than just grocery shop today, Beau." Her eyes bore into his.

He waited—not sure if this was going to be good news or bad.

"I had a doctor appointment, too."

Peggy Patrick

His eyes grew, worry lines instantly creasing his brow. "Why? You're all right, aren't you?"

She nodded as her glowing smile returned. "You're going to be a daddy, Beau. Twice."

It took a few seconds for her words to sink in. "Carly." He whispered her name.

When he saw her eyes fill with tears, he stepped into her and pulled her into a tight hug. He held her tight for a full minute, until the last part of what she'd said registered in his brain. He held her away from him then, enough to see her face.

"Twice? Did you just say twice?"

She laughed, choking on a sob. "A sonogram showed twins."

He gripped her shoulders and moved her back a couple steps. His saucer eyes raked her up and down, lingering on her stomach, then rubbed his flat hand across her middle. For the first time, he noticed that she had a little protruding belly.

"We have two little babies in there, Carly." His expression was pure *dumbfounded*.

She giggled. "Yes, cow-man, I know." She had nicknamed him cow-man soon after they married, letting him know he was more to her than just a cow-*boy*. She would swear he suddenly stood two inches taller the first time she called him that.

His shock turned quickly into a chuckle, then he tilted his head back and laughed with pure joy as he wrapped his arms around her and hugged her close. "Oh, baby girl of mine, how could my life ever be any more blessed?"

"Well, let me think. You *could* prevent having to carry me out of here by moving your boot off my bare sandaled toes."

"What!" He rolled both of his feet sideways, jerking his face down to see what he had stupidly done to her foot. He squatted down and rubbed his hands over her now dirt smudged shoe straps and massaged the exposed tips of her toes. "I'm sorry, Carly. Your news made a wreck out of me. You okay?"

70

"I'm fine, but being as you're *my* wreck, I'll just have to put up with you."

He stood and held her face between his hands. "That's a fact, mam, dern your luck." His kiss was warm and gentle. "So...well...what do we do first?" He still had her face in his hands.

"About what?"

"Having our two babies."

She giggled and pulled his hands away from her face. If she could love a man more than she loved this one, she'd have to be God Himself—the pure fullness of Love. She could see the stress gathering in his eyes. All she wanted to do was kiss that away, but not here.

"We have six whole months to get what they'll need, cow-man.

He stared into space a second, then back to her. "You're already three months?"

She nodded.

His thoughts were arrested then by a loud truck horn sounding from not far away. They both turned in the direction of the barn door.

"Sounds like our rodeoing preacher-man has arrived," Beau quipped.

"Oh good, let's go eat. I'm starved."

Carly was a picky eater and never ate enough to keep a mouse alive. Beau glanced down at her at that declaration. She cut her eyes at him without moving her head. "Three. I'm feeding three of us."

He laughed out loud. "So, you are. Let's go get you...*ya'll* fed."

Hand in hand they headed out and up the drive where everyone was gathered around Andy. By the time they reached the crowd, most of the hugs were done and people were heading toward the pavilion.

Andy saw Beau and Carly approaching and hurried toward them, wrapping them both in a burly bear-hug. He landed a kiss on Carly's cheek, then Beau's.

"Man, it's good to see you two."

"You, too, Andy." Beau looked him up and down. "Dude, I'm glad I already knew you were coming home today or I wouldn't have recognized you. What'd you do...cut your hair?"

Andy rubbed the short, dark stubble and mustache that covered his jaws and upper lip and grinned. "Yeah, I guess I'm a little scruffy looking." He lifted his Stetson straw and raked his longer hair back before replacing the hat. "Granny already threatened to go get a pair of scissors. But you two look great. How are things around here?"

"For as I know, everything's good. I sure hope you're home to stay, though."

"I am. Come on, I'll introduce you to some pretty little friends of mine. They're needing a temporary place to live," was all he offered about them.

Beau nodded and he and Carly followed to the pavilion where the three ladies were undoubtedly already being pampered into ruination.

Andy watched a few seconds as his mom and Granny Martha and Aunt Reeny fussed over the girls. He was more proud right now of this family of his than ever. They asked no questions—They just loved.

As soon as Andy entered the pavilion, little Rachel ran from behind her mother's legs and straight into his arms. She was crying inconsolably and wrapped both arms around his neck, her face buried in the collar of his red chambray shirt. He held her tight, his large hand splayed across her back.

A glance at Summer told him she had no idea what was wrong. Everyone had noticed and turned to watch the little girl cling to Andy.

"Rachel, baby, can you tell me why you're crying," he whispered against her ear. But she gripped him tighter and continued.

He knew she hadn't had anything to eat since noon. Before he could move on that thought, Granny Martha came toward him with a plate of mashed potatoes, fried chicken and fruit salad.

"Sit down and see if she'll eat, Andy." She set the plate on a picnic table while Laura brought a cup of lemonade and silverware.

"Let's bless the food right quick, folks," Jesse announced as he removed his hat. He said a prayer and everyone began filling plates.

Reeny and Carly introduced themselves to Summer and ushered her over to make a plate. That's when Summer turned a circle, searching for Emma Jo. She was nowhere to be seen.

Noticing her frantic look, Grandpa Hank walked up— "Ms. Logan, I'm Hank Walton, better known as Grandpa around here. Your girl is with the Brandon kids. They headed off to the petting zoo. I'll go head 'em back this way. You go ahead and make you a plate."

That's when Summer realized why Rachel was crying. She wasn't used to being without her sister. She still clung to Andy and refused to eat, but he was making good use of the fried chicken anyway.

Summer sat beside Andy and offered to rescue him from her tired, crying baby. But, Rachel was having no part of her mom. She clung even tighter to him. Within another minute, she stopped crying and relaxed her hold. She was sound asleep.

Unsure of the relationship between her son and Summer, Laura waited until all had been fed, then she offered to show his guests to their cabin. Rachel was still in his lap sleeping. He seemed content to hold her while he ate and visited.

This boy of hers had become a man when she wasn't looking. Maybe that was why he'd changed so fast—He wasn't being mothered at every dip in the road. Or, *at all,* for that matter. His phone calls home had been sweet, but not needy—just to say *'hello, I'm still alive and how is everybody.'* He had taken care of his own business, and apparently, taken on the care of a few more. To say she was proud of her son was a bit understated.

Oh, it ouched a little when the apron strings finally detached, but that's common to every mother on God's planet earth.

Still—she wondered if he had brought home a ready-made addition to their family or was Summer Logan just needing help getting established somewhere.

"Thanks, Mom, but I'll get them settled in. Which cabin is theirs?"

She nodded. "The little woodsy one. Thought Summer might like the privacy."

"Perfect. I'll be up to talk to you and Dad after I take them over there."

She patted his broad muscled shoulders that ropers were known for and looked up just as Summer approached with Emma Jo reluctantly in tow.

"Summer, we're so glad you and your girls are here with us. I hope you find the little cabin comfortable."

"Thank you, Mrs. Brandon. Everyone here is so kind." Tears sprang into her eyes and she gave Andy an embarrassed glance.

After repositioning Rachel on his shoulder, he stood and led them back to the truck to drive around to the cabin.

In a few minutes, it would be dark. Andy made sure Summer could see where her cabin set in proportion to where he'd be in the ranch house. He couldn't imagine her being scared out here—not after where she'd been living in the Sawtooth Mountains.

The porch light and interior lamps were on when they opened the door. Emma ran straight to the three-quarter sized rollaway bed in the corner of the living room where a large recliner used to set.

"Mama, look!" She exclaimed and ran to grab one of the baby dolls that sat in the middle of a bright yellow and pink quilted comforter. The shams on two big fluffy pillows matched the bed covering. On the foot of the bed were two pink ruffled night gowns. Emma clutched the dolly in her arms and beamed at the little girls colorful, cheery bedroom that had been cleverly designed into the corner of the den—From a hanging lamp, to wall pictures of lambs and rainbows, to a white, fuzzy throw rug—Andy was flabbergasted. Summer was crying again.

"Wow." It took him a couple minutes to absorb the female cuteness in this cabin before finally depositing little Rachel under the covers that Summer pulled back for her. He stuck the other baby doll close to her and covered them both.

Emma had already toured the rest of the cabin and decided she wanted a shower before getting in the pretty bed.

Andy shook his head. What six-year-old thinks like that!?

"This kitchen and bath are fully stocked, Summer, so help yourself to it and if you need anything, my house number is there by the phone. Don't hesitate to call me." He took her hand in his when she didn't answer. "Promise me you'll ask if you need something."

She squeezed his hand and nodded. "I promise. Andy...I..." She was so overwhelmed at what this family had done for her and her children, she couldn't come up with adequate words.

He smiled, leaned down and kissed her—A warm, lingering caress of his lips that she returned without inhibitions. "I know," he whispered against the side of her mouth. "Get some sleep. I'll see you tomorrow." He left without looking back.

The wind was getting up, not unusual for Wyoming, but the crisp coolness was a change. It felt good blowing on his hot face as he slowly drove back to the ranch house. His bed was going to feel so good after sleeping too many nights in the back seat of his truck. But being able to sleep might prove to be a problem.

Summer Logan. She had blindsided his broken heart. The change came so suddenly that he now wondered what it was that he'd been feeling for Abby Luke. Infatuation? He couldn't even see Abby in his mind's eye now. It was Summer who popped front and center, along with those two precious little girls.

If Abby had been the one God meant for him to marry, Summer wouldn't have been able to change his feelings like this. There was something far more at work in this relationship than anything he'd experienced before. His legs felt weighed down as he walked out of her cabin. He should be there with her. It crossed his mind to sleep on the reclining love seat in the cabin den, but no use in creating a firestorm over this with his family. He just needed to get it figured out soon or he was going to be as worthless as a..."

The aroma of strong fresh brewed coffee stopped his roll of thoughts as he entered the back door into the kitchen of—*home.* Yes, Lord—*home!*

"We're in here, Andy," his mom yelled from the den. "Grab a cup of coffee. We have ours."

Andy blew on the rim of the cup and slurped the best swallow of coffee he'd had in four months as he joined his mom and dad in the little cubby hole den just off the kitchen.

"It's so nice to see you walk in here with coffee in your hand." Laura's smile filled up her mama-eyes.

"Thanks, Mom. It's good to be home."

"Do you still have some rodeos scheduled?" Jesse asked.

He swallowed a hot sip and shook his head. "No. Me and Sugar Beet retired from the road."

It dawned on him then—he was right back in his old situation, living at home like a school kid. That part of being home again didn't feel quite right this time. He was a grown man now and he needed to act like it. So, that made two major life issues that needed dealt with immediately.

"Actually, I'm only going to need to stay here until I can make arrangements to have my own place."

Laura sat up straighter and frowned. "Son, this is your home. You don't have to hurry and move out."

"No, Mom, I *do* need to be independent. You and Dad have done your job with me. I'm not going far. I just have to decide what kind of house I need. Whatever I decide, I'll put it over on my acreage. I've been thinking about this for the past year— Just haven't done anything about it."

Jesse leaned forward in his easy chair, both hands wrapped around his coffee mug. "Andy, does this have anything to do with Ms. Logan—Your need for your own home?"

He was a little taken aback at his dad's direct question. He looked him in the eyes, hesitated, then shook his head. "No, not really. That's another subject, but I do owe you both an explanation about her and the girls."

For the next thirty minutes, he told the story of Summer, Emma Jo and Rachel Logan. "It took about a half a day to get Billie the milk cow and a dozen chickens hauled to town. The pastor of the only little church in town took them and seemed genuinely happy about it. Then, we headed for High Point and…here we are."

Jesse and Laura both sat in silence for a long minute after hearing the details of this young mother's plight. Laura brushed a single tear drop off her cheek. "I'm just so thankful to God that we did the extras in their cabin. If anyone deserved that, those three sure did."

"I saw that girlie little bedroom in there. Emma Jo was so impressed, she wanted a shower before she got in the *pretty bed.*" Andy chuckled after thinking about that for a second.

Jesse watched Andy's expressions when he talked about Summer, as well as the little girls. *Discreet* about his feelings wasn't in the mix.

"So, how serious are you and Summer?" He asked for the second time.

77

Andy stared at the floor, then up at his dad. "Do you believe in love at first sight?"

Jesse smiled. "Happens all the time."

Laura glanced at them both, concern creasing her brow. "Honey, isn't this a little soon after your breakup with Abby?"

The mention of her should have stirred his heart a little bit, at least—It didn't. It almost felt as though she had never happened.

He shook his head. "This is different, Mom. I...can't explain it. It's just...different."

She glanced at Jesse and a knowing twinkle danced between them.

Summer gently pulled back the coverlet on the full bed in her room. She ran her hands over the eyelets cut into the puffy white comforter. She had never seen anything like it. It made her think of a fluffy cloud. She had taken a long, leisure shower, scrubbing her skin until it tingled. She folded the new jeans and T-shirt that Andy had bought her the day they left the state of Idaho. He had stopped at a mall in one of the cities they went through and bought her and both girls a few new clothes and shoes—right down to new under-things.

She looked at the girls once more before turning off her light and sliding between the soft sheets.

It seemed to hit her all at once as she lay staring into the dark shadowy room—the aloneness of being in an unfamiliar place surrounded by people she didn't know and hundreds of miles away from all she knew as home.

But, what had she left behind? A cow and a few chickens? And they didn't even belong to her anymore. Her house was gone. Just an old empty barn remained. She and Andy had loaded most of the hay and grain to take to the preacher in town to help feed Billie and the chickens. After that—well, there was no after that. Except for Andy Parker. And the truth was, she didn't really know Andy Parker.

So, who was he? He was a cowboy who got lost traveling through Idaho and happened onto her tiny speck on the planet to spend the night in her barn. He owned a sweet and beautiful horse and he was a rodeo calf roper. He has an extremely nice family here in Wyoming who owns a dude ranch called High Point. He has a truck and horse trailer that got pummeled by a hail storm.

She stared harder into the now, semi-darkness, seeing Andy's face from her inner vision. He was tall with wide muscled shoulders and sometimes his voice sounded deeper than other times—like when he was talking to Emma Jo or Rachel—then it was soft and so loving. When he spoke to her, it was lower pitched, but so kind. He had provided for every single need she and her children had. She never asked him for anything—He just seemed to know. He had bought them food and clothes. He had protected them from all forms of danger.

The picture she envisioned next brought a smile with it. Andy knew Jesus. He initiated dancing for God and he praised Him aloud while they all danced in front of her destroyed home.

What else did she really need to know about him?

She felt her heartbeat pick up a notch at the roll of memories that turned one after the other through her mind—the gentle, nonjudgmental way he had handed her pistol back to her after she'd threatened him with it, the way he'd taken the liberty to take her girls out of that awful woman's cafe in Forest Valley. She felt the relief all over again as she pictured her babies sleeping in the back seat of his truck.

Not once had he tried to take advantage of her in any way, even when opportunities had presented itself.

Andy was a true gentleman, he loved God and her babies. The way he had held baby Rachel tonight during the outdoor meal, refusing to put her down while he ate or visited with his family. Rachel had clung to him and he comforted her—That stood out to her above everything else.

In many ways, Andy reminded her of Joe Logan, except that Joe never had much patience with the children.

Then, she allowed herself to remember Andy's kiss after he had been cross with her for being inside the wobbly cabin after the storm. And his kiss tonight before leaving this cabin.

A grabbing sensation shot through her middle suddenly and she turned on her side pulling her knees up until she was curled almost in a ball. She wrapped her arms around herself and wondered at the desire that had engulfed her senses.

Andy. She wished he was there with her right now. Andy.

***

CHAPTER SEVEN

"You're up and at em' early." Donny Brandon had come up behind Andy in the barn where he was saddling one of the ranch geldings.

Andy jerked his head around as he pulled the cinch a notch tighter. "Hey, Uncle Donny. Just felt like a ride around the ranch before the place starts hopping."

"Sun won't be up for over an hour. Care for some company?"

"You bet. Saddle up. I could use an opinion besides my own."

In minutes, they headed out past the Cowboy Church building and toward the acres adjoining the dude ranch.

Walking side by side, Andy's peripheral vision watched his uncle stare at the side of his face. Finally, he couldn't stand it.

"What?" Andy turned his face toward him.

Donny laughed. "Sorry dude, but I can't get over your hairy...head. If I'd sat down beside you at the burger joint, I would not have recognized you."

Andy smiled and scratched his whiskered cheek. "Yeah, well it was just easier on the road to let it go. Got kind of used to myself, I guess."

"You just look...older. I'm used to the kid Andy Parker. You went and manned-up on me."

"About time, don't you think.?"

They rode in silence for a few minutes before Andy stopped and slowly turned his horse in a full circle. Donny watched him turn his head to look out in every direction, studying the lay of the land in the partial moonlight.

"Right here, Uncle Donny. This is the spot."

"Okay, that's wonderful, Andy. Spot for what?"

"My new house. This shallow valley we're in is beautiful from top of that hill there. What do you think?"

Donny scanned the area as far as he could see and nodded his head up and down. "Yep. I can see a great little home place set in this spot." He eyed Andy, questions running over each other in his head. "So, what brought this on suddenly? Is there something you haven't told us yet?"

Andy laughed aloud. "Yes and no. First of all, I need to leave the nest. I figured that was long overdue."

"And what's the *second* of all?"

He was quiet, looking down at his hands that rested on the horn of his saddle. "I'm not sure about that part yet."

Donny smiled knowingly. "Do you love her, Andy?"

His head bobbed up and down again. "Yes." He stared at his hands. "I just met her, but I..."

"I get that. You know I do. Just take your time. Get to know each other. She sure is a pretty lady and those little girls stole all our hearts." He watched Andy's face turn from contemplative to pure misery. He had a lot going on in his head. "Andy, when something is meant to be, it'll come around. I believe I heard a

82

young preacher boy say that very thing one Sunday morning a few months back."

Andy looked away as he worked furiously to swallow the lump sitting on his vocal cord. His heart was thundering in his chest. His world had changed from the tight, secure hold of his childhood when he had loaded up four months ago and hit the road. Today it felt as though he was suddenly thrust into another, larger change. He was compelled to build his own home place, he was so in love with a beautiful stranger and already he felt like a daddy to two little girls—And a sermon was burning in his heart that he knew would put him back into the pulpit of the community Cowboy Church. God sure knew how to put a man's britches on a boy—quick!

By the time the sun peaked over the eastern tree line, a couple of cabins and teepee of dudes were out to greet it with stretches and yawns as they ambled toward the chuck wagon.

Grandpa Hank had made sure his breakfast customers were awakened by his loud, jangling *come and get it while it's hot* bell. Of course, he always rang it ten full minutes before the biscuits would be ready.

Donny and Andy had been back just long enough to feed their mounts and head to their respective homes—Donny to get his family and head back for breakfast before he set off to do day work for the Double OO—And Andy to spend a little time with the Lord before getting his plans underway for the day. His final *Thank You* and *Amen* came in perfect sync with the bell ringing, making him chuckle. He heard the rest of the house stirring, taking their ten minutes to get out the door. It was good to be home.

"Was that you that made that noise, Mister?"

Hank's back was turned to the small voice behind him, but it didn't startle him in the least. He was used to people of all sizes sneaking around the food wagon. He turned to find a little girl not waist high starring up at him. Even though her long, thick, dark-brown, curly hair was loose and wadded all over her head and shoulders, he recognized her. Her ponytail from last evening couldn't change those huge, beautiful brown eyes partially hidden in her messy hair now.

"Well, good morning, Miss Emma. Yes, mam, I'm guilty of making that noise."

"I'm Emma *Jo*. So why did you do that?"

"That's my breakfast bell, Emma *Jo,* and you're my first customer. You must be hungry."

She nodded vigorously.

"Well, let me get you a plate fixed and you can dig in."

She graced him with a wide smile then, that turned his old heart to mush, especially when those big browns twinkled up at him.

He carried her plate to a picnic table and handed her a plastic fork.

"Thank you very much," she chirped and went to town on the bacon.

"Lord, you're so good to this old man," he muttered with a joyful chuckle. Hank had never had a child of his own, and yet, he had them all over the ranch. Most of them, including the visiting little dudes, called him Grandpa.

"Morning, Hank."

"Hey, Hank."

"Morning Beau. Carly. Biscuits are piping hot. Grab a plate there and I'll fill it up for you."

Carly was first in line, grabbing a bite with her fingers before Hank could get her plate filled. He grinned at her. "This girls got an appetite. Don't believe I've ever seen you so hungry."

"Never know—maybe she's eating for two these days," Reeny joked as she grabbed up a plate and held it out to Hank.

"Three," Carly said without looking up, then fingered an extra piece of bacon from the serving pan before heading to a seat in the pavilion.

Hank and Reeny both froze for several seconds, staring after her, then at each other.

"Did she say...?"

"Three?" Hank finished Reeny's question.

Despite the rising volume of the breakfast crowd, the small child's screams and wails that were heavy with real fear or pain arrested everyone's attention. The tiny girl with a tousled head of long dark curls that most women could only wish they owned, was running toward the pavilion from the far end of the drive. She was barefoot, but otherwise, fully dressed. A baby doll was grasped in her little fist.

Beau had jumped up and reached her first, scooping her up to try and see where her pain was. Was something biting her? But she fought him, still screaming until he set her back on her feet.

"I'm just right here, Rachel." Emma Jo sounded a little put out as she took her sister's hand and pulled her along to the pavilion. The wailing immediately stopped, drawing smiles and chuckles from the group of people—including Beau.

Jesse, Laura and Andy had all piled out of the ranch house at the same time—Andy having already announced that who they were hearing was Rachel.

Noticing that Granny Martha had already set a plate in front of Rachel and that Summer was nowhere to be seen, Andy headed straight for her cabin to check on her.

Summer opened her eyes and blinked several times before she remembered. Wow! She couldn't recall having slept that sound since before having her first baby. She reached over and pulled the mini blind apart enough to know that the sun was already high up—And to notice Andy walking into the clearing and toward her cabin. She jumped up and ran into the bathroom for twenty seconds worth of brushing her teeth. By then, she heard the knocking. She stepped inside the doorway to the den and realized Andy was already inside and knocking on the wall. In the same moment, her peripheral vision had caught the empty bed where her girls had slept, and the realization that the front door was pushed open all the way to the wall.

The fearful expression that crossed her face caused Andy to put up a hand. "Don't get excited. The girls are fine. They're having breakfast with the rest of the crew. I came down to check on you."

She nodded. "I'm fine, I just slept too hard. I didn't even know my babies were gone. I'm…usually a better mother than this."

"Hey," he pushed the door shut and walked over to her. "You are a very good mother, Summer. Those little rascals are in a new place and with all the attention they're getting, they're just excited."

"I know, but they still have to have some boundaries and be mindful of it."

"Yes, mam, they do. See, that's what I mean. You have good parenting skills. They just need to know what their new boundaries are in this new place. This is all different for them and for you."

He gently raked her jumbled hair back and cupped her face with his hands to look full into those innocent, widened eyes. He studied her face for several long seconds, feeling a fire beginning to kindle. His heart pounded hard in his chest until he thought it might explode any second. "Little girl," he growled a warning more to himself than to her, "if you don't want this cowboy to eat you all up, you'd better step away from me now."

When she leaned toward him, returning the longing all the way into her gold flecked pools—it was all over. He moaned under his breath as he wrapped an arm around her. He pulled her head against his shoulder and kissed her hard and fevered, grasping a wad of her hair in a tight fist. He kissed her until they were both breathless.

Summer was sure her legs wouldn't hold her up if he turned her loose. Never had she felt what she was feeling now in Andy's arms—warm, shaky, intoxicated, weak in the knees—and wanting him to lock the cabin door and make love to her.

She pulled back then until he finally loosened his hold. She went to the door and slid the lock in place.

He inhaled a deep breath and let it out slowly. He had started something here that he couldn't finish. There was a time he would not have hesitated to just enjoy the pleasures of the moment, but not now.

For two reasons, when she came back to him, he grasped her upper arms and held her away from him just enough to let them both calm down.

He was not going to disrespect the vow he'd spoken to God, to follow His Commands each day—and he wasn't going to disrespect Summer Logan.

He had walked into this cabin and mindlessly let this happen. What was he thinking? He *wasn't* thinking. He was feeling and he knew he was going to have to figure out how to explain his stupidity to her and then keep his distance—or marry her!

"Andy, is something wrong?"

He studied her for several seconds before answering. "Yes, something's wrong—and something's right." He ran his hands up and down her bare upper arms. He thought he should feel uncomfortable standing here with her in the skimpy little knee length cotton gown she had picked out for herself when they went clothes shopping. But there was nothing uncomfortable about it. In fact, this is what felt so *right*. This is where he belonged. He knew that as well as he knew his own name. But things between him and Summer had to progress the proper way—proper in God's Eyes. He wasn't sure she even knew that

God had rules about sex before marriage. This day and time, most people didn't care.

She stood still, unsure what to do. She felt embarrassed, but mostly confused. "What happened? I...I thought when you said you...well, wanted to eat me up...that you wanted..."

He couldn't hold it. A bubble of laughter burst in his throat and he lowered his face, trying to get control. "Oh, man alive," he finally muttered. He pulled her to him and planted a quick kiss on her lips. He could feel the contour of her body, the flimsy material concealing nothing. "Believe me, sweet girl, I *do* want to. But that can't happen like this. I shouldn't have come in this way. I guess I didn't expect you to take me that literal."

She backed up out of his reach and folded her arms across her middle. "So, you didn't really mean it."

"Oh—I meant it, but..."

"But, you want to be married first?"

Face value was a mild way to describe this lady. There was a riveting pause as his gaze held hers. "God wants it that way, Summer." His voice had dropped off to just more than a whisper.

She nodded up and down. "I better get dressed and see about my girls."

His mouth of saliva went down hard. "all right."

She turned and disappeared around the door frame into her bedroom.

He shuffled slowly to the front door and left. *Had a bigger idiot ever been born?* He felt like that word was written across his forehead in flashing neon. He knew he'd done the right thing in the end, but never in his wildest did he expect that response from Summer.

He inhaled a deep breath and tried to calm himself as he walked back to the pavilion. Most had already eaten and Grandpa Hank and Granny Martha were busy cleaning up. The girls were nowhere to be seen.

"Andy!"

He wheeled around to see Grandpa Hank waving him over to the chuck wagon.

"What's up, Gramps? Know where the little girls went?"

"They're in the barn with your mom and dad. Here—" he handed two filled breakfast plates to him, "might be a bit cold, but still good. You and Ms. Logan's the only ones that didn't eat."

"Thanks, Gramps." As he carried the plates to the pavilion, his mom emerged from the barn leading Buddy with Emma Jo and Rachel both sitting in the seat of the saddle. Emma had a death grip with both hands on the horn, while Rachel was about to squeeze the life out of Emma—her arms so tight around her waist, they almost melded into one girl.

Andy grinned and waved as the troop passed by him looking like they were being punished for something. And knowing his mother, she wouldn't stand for a kid on this ranch being scared to ride a dead-broke pony.

Summer took in everything along the drive as she walked toward the beautiful picnic area. She noticed how each cabin was set beneath its own canopy of pine trees and none of them looked alike. Each had a different size and shape of porch or front entrance. But it was the semicircle of Indian teepees on the opposite side of the drive and set back a ways that stopped her in her tracks. *An Indian village?* She started to head over to see them up close when a shrill whistle grabbed her attention. Andy was waving her over to a picnic table so she headed that way.

"Gramps saved you some breakfast. Come on, I'll eat with you."

She sat across from him, still darting her eyes around the grounds.

"The girls are getting a pony ride. They're with my mom."

"Yes, I saw them come out of the barn. They looked scared, but your mama looked like she knew what she was doing."

"*That* she does. They'll be fine with her."

Summer bit into her biscuit with gusto. She was starved. "Is that... a real Indian village over there." She swallowed and scooped up a bite of scrambled egg.

He thought she sounded truly interested in the Indian teepees, but she was deliberately avoiding making eye contact with him.

"Yes, it's made to look like one. Those teepees are fully furnished for our ranch guests who want that type of lodging. The kids really like to stay in them."

She kept her eyes on her food as she ate. "I'd love to go see them."

"Soon as we're finished here, I'll give you the grand tour of the whole ranch."

"Thank you." She smiled halfheartedly without looking up.

He concentrated on eating the food in front of him that he didn't want. He had really messed things up with his little macho cowboy act. Except it wasn't an act. Far from it. He simply hadn't realized the full extent of Summer's trusting innocence. She was so much like a child in her acceptance of words spoken to her or actions directed at her. She was refreshingly naive in worldly *smarts*. She needed time—Had so much growing to do, and yet she had two small children that needed more than she could give them alone.

And what kind of idiot, knowing as much about her as he did, would set her up to be—embarrassed...

Oh, my Jesus! It just hit him. That's what's wrong with her. *I embarrassed her. She can't even look at me.*

While he carried their plates to the trash, she stared out at the teepees and waited.

He hurried back and grasped her hand, walking faster than necessary as he pulled her along behind him. He went straight to the honeymoon teepee that faced away from the view of the ranch yard and opened the wooden door concealed behind the large flap of leather. He pulled her inside and closed the door.

The big bed with soft white fluffy coverings like the one in her cabin, and red and turquoise pillows and rugs had her spell bound from the minute she saw them. She knew Andy had something heavy on his mind, hauling her in here this way, but she was trying to see everything and process this other world she'd just stepped into.

This teepee looked like something she might see in one of the magazines in the grocery store. It was beautiful, right down to pots of cactus with yellow flowers blooming on them. She walked over and touched a petal, realizing immediately that it wasn't real. The cactus needles were soft, but they *looked* real. They were beautiful. This teepee was fit for a princess. She'd never imagined anything like this.

Andy watched her, intrigued at her reaction to this interior—the pure awe and wonder of a child. Yet, she was far from a child in all the ways that counted. What a rare little jewel his Summer was.

His Summer. They were from two different worlds. He knew just enough about life to know he needed to size–up and discern nearly everything that moved around him. She knew just enough to let herself or her children get hurt by trusting too easily.

She still had not looked at him.

"Summer."

Her back was to him, but the way he said her name made her fully aware of him. She couldn't bring herself to turn around. What he must think of her after acting like she did. He had laughed at her.

Her breath caught when she felt his hands gently settle around her waist from behind. He turned her to face him and waited for her to look at him. Finally, she did and tears filled her eyes.

"Summer," he whispered. "I'm so sorry I made you feel ashamed. That's what these tears are, aren't they?"

"You laughed and I...I..."

"Honey, I wasn't laughing at what you did. Oh, geez…I was flattered out of my boots. I laughed because you make me feel so happy inside. You're like a breath of fresh air to me—sweet, clean, pure air."

She lowered her head, not sure she believed him.

"I mean that, baby. Please look at me." He waited. "Summer."

Finally, she raised her head after swiping the spilled drops off her cheeks. "I don't know what to do now, Andy. I don't…know how to fit in."

"I do. I know what you should do."

She studied his face that went from a tense concern to a relaxed smile that was aimed straight into her soul.

"Marry me."

She felt the ground move beneath her feet and she swooned at his words—His hands tightened slightly on her waist. Shock and excitement fought for prominence in her brain.

Finally, after a long struggling moment—"Do you love me?" She spoke soft and low.

He squeezed her hard for emphasis. "More than just *that*. I do love you. But, I'm so *in love* with you, I can't think straight. I'm running around here like a demented fool. I can't think of anything except you and how much I love you, Summer. I want you for my wife, my best friend, my lover, my babies' mother. Help me out here, will you?"

Her smile grew as he piled on the titles to her place in his life. "And…I can cook up a storm," she added.

Andy burst into laughter. "My lord, girl, you're killing me. So…was that…" he couldn't stop the chuckles, "a yes?"

Her broad smile turned to a giggle then. "Yes, that was a *yes,* because I'm in love with you, too, Andy Parker, and I want to have babies for you."

He could literally see her heart shining openly in her eyes and knew she meant it.

His eyes were telling her that he was truly in love with her. She put her arms around his neck and when he pressed his lips to hers—he knew this was going to be the shortest engagement he could possibly make happen.

"When?" She whispered against his mouth.

"As soon as we get our home ready. We don't want to start off needing to be taken care of by my...*our* family."

Family. He was giving her something she never expected to have. A whole family with parents and grandparents and cousins for her girls—sisters in law and brothers in law.

She recalled something then that Joe had told her once—*If we praise God every day, He will always take care of us!* Could that be why Andy got lost and drove up her mountain road that night?

"Where will our home be?"

"*That,* my lady, is our next stop on the tour. Come on, let's take a jeep ride. If the girls are back from their ride, we'll take them with us."

Ten minutes later, Andy and his little family were headed through the pasture in Jesse's jeep. He pointed out Beau and Carly's house set back into the trees, then the church. Donny and Reeny's log house could be seen in the distance before the ground dropped off into a beautiful valley.

Finally, he stopped, seemingly out in the middle of nowhere. No houses could be seen in either direction—just acres of beautiful grass and a thick array of multicolored wild flowers.

"Can we pick flowers, Mama?" Emma Jo leaned out over the side from the back seat.

"Sure, that would be fun." Summer got out and helped Emma over the side of the topless jeep.

Andy swung Rachel high in the air as he lifted her out, making her squeal and giggle. He loved hearing that sound.

In another moment, he raced around the front of the vehicle, grasped Summer's hand and pulled her a few yards out into the flowery field. "Right here! Look around you, Summer. That's what you'll see from the windows of our house."

She turned herself in a circle, noticing the tree line on the farthest side and along the back. But the trees were quite a way off. It was wide open—a sense of calm and freedom engulfed her. The beauty of belonging somewhere meshed with the physical beauty of the land she stood on. She knew she truly *did* belong here—with Andy Parker. They would raise her girls right here on this piece of Heaven on earth. And she and Andy would make more babies.

Suddenly she wanted to dance across this little valley and shout praises to the Lord Jesus. Somehow, that would set this whole plan in stone in her mind.

Andy was watching her reaction, not even surprised when she raised her arms and her face toward Heaven and began to twirl in circles. She thanked God aloud for his Goodness to her new family. After a moment, she grasped his hand and together they danced before the Lord and worshipped Him.

***

CHAPTER EIGHT

"Where is she?" Judd Luke bellowed as he entered the mud room at the back door of his and Toni's spacious log home.

Toni hadn't seen anger on her husband like this since before they were married over twenty years ago. She rushed out of the kitchen toward him in an attempt to run interference.

"Honey, calm down before you say things you'll regret."

"Of all the asinine, ridiculous, senseless reasons to up and leave school. She's throwing away her entire education, not to mention several thousand dollars of tuition. That girl's I.Q. is higher than mine and yours put together and all she's talked about is college and law school for years now."

"Judd, I rode out to the back ninety earlier to tell you this so you'd have time to digest it before you got home. You know I don't like wasting my time, so simmer down. This isn't going to help anybody." She went to him and put her hand on the small of his back.

He pushed the brim of his sweat stained Stetson higher on his forehead and sucked a deep breath.

"Anyway—I *know* there's more to this story than what she told me. We have to give her time to let us in on it. She's up in her room."

"Did she just...*quit?*"

"It doesn't sound like she plans to go back."

"Did you tell her that Andy is involved with someone now?"

Toni shook her head and moved around in front of Judd to look him in the eyes. "No, I didn't and I think we need to let her find that out without our help."

He stared down at the floor in silence for a minute as he forced himself to take a step back emotionally. "All right. And I do believe you're right about there being more to this than she's saying. Quitting school and coming home because she missed Andy is just not cuttin' it."

"Well, I'm going to make supper and lets just be calm about this until we know more."

"I'll go up and see her." He took off his hat and hung it on a peg before heading to wash his hands in the kitchen sink—He headed upstairs.

At the familiar sound of her dad's jangling spurs coming up the stairs, Abigail swung open her door and rushed into his arms before he reached her room.

"Daddy!" She burst into tears and sobbed loudly with her face in his shirt front.

Bewildered, Judd embraced her, his arms tightening as she sobbed harder. For the first time today since he learned his daughter had shut down her dreams of law school and returned home—he felt afraid.

Hearing the cries of her normally unemotional daughter, Toni had rushed to the den and stopped at the bottom of the stairs. She stood still, looking up at the unusual scene between father and daughter and let her own tears run unchecked down her cheeks. *What has happened to our Abby?*

One Week Later

Everything was happening so fast, falling into place for Andy and Summer's new home and wedding plans. They talked endlessly about details, secured the same home builders that Donny and Reeny used and set things privately into motion.

Opting to spend more money on building their new home place, they decided to forgo all the wedding glitter. New clothes for everyone to wear for the ceremony and a casual reception in the pavilion was the final plan. Breaking the *casual* part to his mom and Granny Martha was the only rough place Andy anticipated. Get that part over with and they would be home free!

Andy's large, warm hand clasped Summer's small thin fingers as he led her into the enclosed patio just outside the back door of his family's ranch house. Rachel was balanced on his other arm while Emma Jo walked close beside him.

"Come on in and find a chair." Jesse greeted each one as Laura passed out hugs before heading inside for a snack tray—coffee brewed on the patio coffee bar.

After the girls had cookies and juice served at their own table, and coffee cups filled for the rest, Andy made the announcement.

"Mom, Dad...I've asked this gorgeous woman here to become my wife." He slipped his hand around her forearm. "She said 'yes'. Then, I asked those two munchkins over there if I could be their daddy and they said 'yes' and 'Anny daddy.' He grinned. "I took that as a yes. And we wanted you two to be the first to know."

Laura put her fingers over her mouth to cover her trembling chin. "Oh, Andy! Summer!" She got up and walked behind their chairs and group hugged them from the back.

Jesse stood and stepped to his son. Andy stood up and the two hugged and back slapped each other. He leaned down and hugged Summer. "Welcome to our family, Ms. Summer."

Once they were all seated again, Emma Jo walked up and wiggled herself in-between Jesse's knees. She looked up into his face. "Hey, Mister, I never had a paw-paw before, but Andy said you was going to be my paw-paw."

By the look on Jesse's face, it hadn't had time to occur to him that he was acquiring a couple of grandchildren. He picked her up and set her on his lap. "Know what, Emma Jo?"

She shook her head as she kept her eyes glued to his.

"I've never been anybody's paw-paw before. So, you will be the very first one to call me Paw-Paw."

Her eyes grew. She smiled ear to ear and clapped her hands in pure joy. "And Rachel, too?"

Rachel was still at the table working on her pile of cookies, oblivious to all the *firsts* that were happening.

"And Rachel, too," Jesse answered, his eyes damp and twinkling.

Laura watched and listened to the exchange between Jesse and Emma Jo. Her heart was near bursting with thankfulness to God for this moment. Her and Jesse's first grandchildren had just come into their lives suddenly, pre-ceremony to make it legal, and the joy of it was indescribable.

"If I'm your paw-paw, who would this lady here beside me be?" He winked at Laura.

Emma looked at her and giggled. "She's my maw-maw, silly head."

Everybody laughed and Emma jumped down and rejoined her sister for another cookie.

"So, when do we need to get going on wedding plans?" Laura was hoping it wouldn't be long months away. Her planning mind was already in high gear.

"That's just the thing, Mom. We've decided on a simple ceremony and reception here just among family and our friends from the Double OO. Our money is going into a new home that, by the way, will be getting underway in the morning."

"Oh, my!" Laura was surprised at how fast these kids were moving forward.

"Tomorrow?" Jesse coughed when his swallow of coffee went down sideways.

"We would like to show ya'll where we are building. Summer likes the idea of a small log cabin. I've got her talked into one a *little* larger—like four bedrooms."

Jesse chuckled. "Sounds like you two have been planning this a while."

"Only since last week. We want our lives to get started without the long engagement or big to-dos for a wedding. Just plain and simple."

Laura eyed Summer, looking for a sign of disappointment. "Summer, do we need to go shopping for a wedding dress, at least?"

"Well," she hesitated, "I was looking at some magazine pictures for weddings when Andy and I went to town the other day and I think I'd like for me and my girls to dress alike in these pretty dresses I found. I want them to feel like they are as much a part of this new life as I am."

Laura let out a breath and leaned back in her chair. "Wow, you two have got this thing under control. That sounds so awesome and...just plain sweet, Summer. Exactly my kind of wedding."

A flush pinked her face as she caught her cowboy of two decades slanting his eyes at her. She knew they were thinking the same thing.

Peggy Patrick

Laura and Jesse's *wedding* had topped the charts for *simple* when he had tapped on her High Point guest cabin window, placed a stool under it and helped her climb out in her night gown to elope with him to the Double OO for a late-night ceremony—Judd Luke officiating and Toni as witness. Their honeymoon was spent in the Luke's guest house by a small lake—three days and nights of pure young love bliss.

Jesse reached over, took her hand and squeezed, bringing a swell of tears and a broad smile.

Andy was watching his mom and dad—sensing what they were reminiscing about. He had heard their story in detail more than once and looked at pictures of his mom climbing out of the window—compliments of Jesse's secret photographer hiding in the dark behind a tree—Granny Martha. This was the favorite story of the Brandon household.

Simple and fun was Andy and Summer's chosen motto for everything they did together. He supposed it was in his blood! For Summer—it was all she knew.

For the next couple of days, Laura and Granny Martha kept Summer occupied with the plans for reception food and cake—but mostly getting to know each other with family stories—some funny, some sad.

Reeny Brandon and Carly Vance got in on parts of the two-day regalia. Even Grandpa Hank sat in on some of the story telling. His offerings were the cherry topping, keeping the women in stitches with his *male* side of the stories. Martha continuously straightened out his story, accusing him of telling it all *backards and down side up!*

The children entertained each other, Anna Leigh Brandon watching over the younger ones.

Up to now, Summer had timidly clung to Andy. The only time she wasn't beside him was when she stayed in her cabin. But, she felt such a oneness with this family now—their love and acceptance was powerful and genuine. She thought this must surely be how Heaven will feel. She couldn't imagine anything better.

While the other men from High Point had hired out for day–work on the Double OO, Andy worked with the home builder to get the cabin staked out. According to the contractor, the house would go up in short order.

Toward the end of the day, Andy sat in the jeep in deep thought imaging his little family living in this beautiful valley in their home—a barn full of horses and kittens and a couple of pups.

"Hello, Andy."

The voice was unmistakable and shook him out of his day dream with a jolt. He turned to find Abby sitting astride Little John, her aged bay gelding that she had grown up with.

He got out of the jeep and stared up at her like he might be seeing a ghost. "Abby. What are you doing here?"

She dismounted, dropped the reins and walked up close to him, acting as though she expected his arms to go around her. When he didn't move, she stood on tiptoes and reached hers around his neck. She planted a kiss on his lips, surprised and a little hurt that he didn't respond.

He reached up and unlocked her arms from around him and took a step back.

"Andy? Aren't you glad to see me? I'm home…to stay."

"Why? When did you come back?"

"Last week. I…wasn't feeling well, so I stayed home. But, I'm better now. I was so anxious to see you."

"I'm sorry, but glad you're better. What happened to school?"

"Oh, I just couldn't decide what I really wanted to do. It didn't feel right, so here I am."

"Abby…"

"I know. I so owe you an apology. I handled things between us badly and I truly am sorry." She looked out at the stakes and materials laying in the field. "So, what's all this? Are you building something?"

"A home."

"Oh, Andy, this is a beautiful spot for a home." She craned her neck trying to see the papers laying on the seat. "Are those the blueprints? Can I look at them, please?"

After a half minute of his silent hesitation, Abby suddenly threw her arms around his middle and pressed the length of her body into his. With the side of her face pressed into his T-shirted chest, she squeezed a tight hug, waiting and expecting to feel his arms come around her.

Instead, his large hands grasped her shoulders and urged her to let him go and step back. When she did, she jerked her face up to his—The hurt that he saw etched there went deep. He hated that he was the cause of it. It hurt his soul to see it—but there were no skipped beats in his heart, no urge to wrap her up and hold her—or kiss her. Nothing. He only realized at that moment that he hadn't thought of her since the day he laid eyes on Summer Logan. Not once could he recall her crossing his mind. He had to tell her.

"Abby...you need to know that there's someone else in my life now."

Her gaze fell to the ground, disbelief coating her face, then slowly she looked back at Andy. "Is it *that* serious?"

"I'm building this house for her. We're getting married."

She stood there letting the shock wash over her. *He can't be serious.* "But...Andy...we've been together all our lives. And we...just before I left for college...we..."

"I'm sorry, Abby. You and I practically grew up in each other's back yards. But...we were never meant to become life partners."

"How do you know that? You're making a mistake, Andy."

"Abby, we loved each other, but it wasn't the kind of love that happens when you find the one God chose for you."

Her saucer blues bore into him for a long moment, not so much from hurt, but anger.

He understood the range of emotions that runs through a person in this circumstance. He had experienced the full gamut for months after she'd broken up with him. So, it didn't surprise him to see her spin on her heel, mount up and take off at a full run.

He stood still for a few moments, not looking up to watch her ride away. Part of him wanted to think she had this coming to her. She was reaping what she'd sowed—but he knew that was his human nature, his *flesh,* as the Bible refers to it, that was doing the thinking. In truth, he believed God's Hand was in all the circumstances concerning him and Abby—The sudden breakup months ago, as painful as it was, and the way he was led to find Summer and her girls. He knew God loved Abby as much as He loved him and He would see her through this—lead her to find *the* one He has for her.

He slid behind the wheel and spun the jeep around, more anxious than ever to see his sweet Summer's face. He couldn't keep from smiling at the thought of her.

Within days, the sides of the cabin were going up. This construction crew meant business—From dawn to dusk, they hardly slowed down. It was what this particular company was known for and much to Andy and Summer's delight, they were true to form.

They began to choose appliances and floor tile and furniture for each room. It was coming together so fast, they finally set a date for their marriage ceremony.

The only real issue—Andy wasn't sure Pastor Judd would be comfortable officiating. He hadn't seen Abby since that day. In fact, he hadn't seen any of the Luke's except for Sunday morning services at Cowboy Church. He hadn't been asked to deliver a sermon since he got back from his rodeo venture—It was just as well, with all that was happening in his world. But he did notice that Abby had not attended church since she got home from college.

With the house now no more than two weeks til turnkey, Andy and Summer decided to have their wedding this coming Saturday evening—mainly because the weather forecast was promising the first winter cold front was on its way down. It was due to blow in dry, but windy and cold by Monday of next week. So, Saturday was the big day. That gave two days to put it together.

Summer had baked her own rendition of chocolate pie, anxious for Andy's parents to try her culinary skills and to hopefully help smooth out the nearly overnight wedding date they were about to throw on them.

"Saturday!" Laura sat straight up like she'd just realized she was late for a meeting. "This is Wednesday and you want a wedding on Saturday?"

"How's the pie? Good, huh?" Andy quipped.

"It's better than good. It's great, and stop trying to soft-soap me." Laura took a sip of her coffee.

Andy couldn't keep from laughing. "Mom, there's not much more to do than invite a few people over to eat supper and wedding cake."

She stared at him as though she was considering what he'd just said.

"He's right, Mrs. Brandon," Summer said politely. "I can make up the potato salad and whatever other dishes we need. I..."

"No, honey, I won't hear of that. There's two things here— This is your wedding day and no matter how simple the festivities, I won't hear of you cooking for that. And the second thing is I would love for you to call me Laura—Or you can call me 'Mom' if you feel like it."

"Thank you. That means a lot to me."

She didn't indicate which name she would use, but Laura could see her about-to-be little daughter-in-law was genuinely touched by what she'd said.

"Alright," Laura started pulling in all the previous conversation the family had discussed earlier on "...so Reeny has volunteered to make a wedding cake and a special ice cream punch. Grandpa Hank and Jesse are smoking a brisket and Granny Martha and I are doing potato salad and beans. We'll pick up the phone and call everybody to let them know they have til Saturday to do their thing and issue invitations the same way. So is there..."

A loud knock on the kitchen door turned everybody's heads around toward it.

Jesse jumped up and swung it open. "Pastor Judd Luke, come on in and join this coffee and pie party. Apparently, we're having a wedding this Saturday evening. You need to be in on this."

It was immediately obvious that something was wrong. Judd stood in the door not trying to hide his displeasure at something.

"I'm looking for Andy," he said, as he stared him straight in the face.

Andy stood, confused and clueless. "Is something wrong?"

"Come outside. We need to visit." Judd turned and quickly walked away from the door.

"I'll be back in a minute," Andy said, giving Summer a squeeze on her shoulder as he went past her.

Judd went to his dually parked down the drive away from the house.

Andy followed. A feeling that something horrible had happened was tying a knot in his belly. When they both reached the far side of the truck, Judd turned a hot glare on him.

"Is my daughter pregnant with *your* baby?"

A fist in his jaw wouldn't have shocked him a bit more than those words. It took a few long seconds before he could absorb the shock enough to speak.

"Abby's...pregnant?"

Judd's eyes narrowed to slits. "Are you saying you didn't know that?"

"No, sir, I didn't know."

"Did she come to see you a few days ago—Rode her horse over here to talk to you?"

"Yes, sir, she did."

"And you're still going to tell me you don't know about the baby?"

"She didn't tell me that, Judd."

His lips compressed. "Somebody is lying."

Andy couldn't make himself tell this angry father that his little daughter is a liar. He shook his head and stood silent. *Abby...having a baby? Judd thinks it's mine. Did she actually say I'm the father? What in the...*

Judd slapped a hand hard onto the truck fender. "Do you have *nothing* to say, Andy? She says she's four and a half months. She said it's your baby."

Stricken with the thought of his happy young life blowing up in his face—and feeling the squeeze of being caught in the crossfire between this father and daughter—who happen to be not only the oldest and dearest friends of his family, but his pastor and senior partner in ministry—he froze. *And* this was Abby, the girl he grew up with and loved. He still loved her—just not... Why was this happening? Why now?

He tried to find the right words, but nothing came.

Without looking at him, Judd stated in a quieter, controlled tone, "I wouldn't be making any wedding plans this weekend." He got in his dually and left.

The initial shock had worn off as Andy watched the tail end of Judd Luke's dually disappear.

Four and a half months? If that was true, then he calculated that she had to have gotten pregnant as soon as she left for school. *How on earth...?*

He didn't move from where he stood, but after a long minute, lowered his face and prayed, *Father in Heaven, we've got us a real big problem this time. You know the truth about all of this, so I'm laying Abby and all concerned in Your Hands. Father, show me how I need to handle this. In Jesus Name, I thank You. Amen.*

After a minute or so, he slowly walked back to the house. All eyes turned on him. "Everything's fine." He stopped behind Summer's chair and covered her slight shoulders with his oversized hands. "Summer and I have some things to talk about, so guess we'll say goodnight. Mom, would you keep the girls corralled for a little longer. They're playing in Anna Leigh's room."

"Sure will." She squinted her eyes up at her son. He looked troubled. "Are you sure there's nothing wrong?"

"Absolutely, Mom. We'll visit later."

Summer attempted to clear dishes from the table, but Laura promptly shooed her and Andy out the door.

Jesse was staring at Laura like bad news had just been reported.

"What?"

"That's what I'm wondering—*What?*"

She went to him and bent to kiss him on the lips. Before she knew what happened, he had her squealing on his lap, her head resting in the crook of his arm—He kissed her like they had just reached their honeymoon destination. Just as she reached her arm around his neck, they both broke up in laughter at the shrill—" Mom! Daddy! Yuck. What's next around here!"

Anna Leigh, at age fourteen, was just old enough to be mortified. She'd seen plenty of hugs and kisses between her parents her whole life—But they supposed their position at the breakfast bar was a little much for her budding puberty.

They separated, but it was long enough for their embarrassed teen to roll her eyes and storm off before they stopped their giggles and chuckles.

Andy drove Summer out to their new home. When they climbed out of the jeep, he took her hand and led her inside, flipped on the recessed lights over the center kitchen bar, then pointed at the two-butt leather recliner, as Beau Vance called it, that was already sitting in the den area of the open floor plan. "We need to talk," he said quietly.

She tried to size him up, as she made her way to the chair, sensing something was coming that she might not want to hear. She had felt the tightness in the air when Pastor Judd had come to the Brandon's door.

He sat down beside her and told her everything of the past year and a half.

"I honestly thought I was in love with her, Summer. That whole year we spent together every day...When she told me she was going to leave for college—take summer classes before the fall semester, she also broke up with me at that same time. It was as if there had been nothing between us. I was devastated—stopped preaching and just left home and made rodeo after rodeo until the day I got on that little mountain trail of a road and wound up at your place. You know the story from there."

She was silent a minute. "So...I'm gathering that Pastor Judd's visit a little while ago has something to do with all this? With his daughter?"

He nodded. "It has everything to do with what I'm working up to tell you."

She looked at him apprehensively, waiting.

"She rode her horse over here about two weeks ago. She said she changed her mind about school and thought we would pick up where we had left off. I told her about you and she left."

"And...her father came to find you...for what reason?"

"He said Abby was four and a half months pregnant and she told him the baby was mine." He held his breath, bracing for an explosion of some kind—that never came.

Instead, she reached and rubbed her small calloused palm back and forth over the back of his dark tanned hand.

"Is it?" She whispered gently.

"No."

"You're that positive?"

"Summer, first off, I want you to know something. I thought I had fallen in love with Abby Luke—until I laid eyes on you the first time. I quickly learned the difference in loving someone verses being *in* love with someone. There's a big difference. I was never *in* love with Abby.

She raised his hand to her mouth and kissed it. "I know the difference, too, Andy. I loved Joe. He gave me my girls and took care of us the best he could. But...I've never felt like this with him—the way you make me feel when we touch or just when I'm alone and thinking about you."

Looking down at their hands that seemed to be making love with each other, she smiled, then giggled.

Andy grinned, loving the sound of her laugh. "What's so funny Miz Summer Rain Logan—almost Parker?"

I just had the craziest thought. It was almost a picture in my mind just now of Adam and Eve—of a rib floating out of his chest and it suddenly turned into Eve."

She turned her face up to look into those eyes that spoke his love so loudly to her and he kissed her as if there would be no tomorrow for another chance.

When he raised his head, he smiled and said, "You have no idea what you just said. Not that we needed it, but you were just shown a clear confirmation from our Father that you are my rib."

A blank expression settled on her face. "What does that mean?"

"It means that you were designed for me and me for you. God chose you and me to become one together in this life."

She thought about that a minute. *"That* must be why you ended up on my mountain road that night...and why I really wanted to run jump in your arms that morning I first saw you, instead of shoot you...with my unloaded gun."

Andy burst out laughing. "Lady...I *cannot,* for the life of me, see myself without you. You *are* the sugar in my tea."

A grin covered her face. "Thank you. I'm really happy about that."

"And...one other thing I want you to know—Abby's baby cannot be mine because we never had sex together. Not once!"

***

CHAPTER NINE

After picking up Emma Jo and Rachel and getting all three ladies settled into their cabin for the night, Andy sat down with Jesse and Laura to give them a heads up.

Before he could broach the subject of Abby and Judd Luke, his dad did it for him.

"Andy," Jesse leaned forward off his recliner, hands clasped, his elbows resting on his spread knees, "I had a phone call after you left. I'd like for you to answer one question for me and your mom—yes or no, if you don't mind."

"All right, I can do that."

"Is there any possibility at all that Abby Luke is pregnant with your baby?"

"No."

The unperturbed, peaceful expression on Andy's face with his simple and quiet *no,* made this issue a done deal as far as his parents were concerned.

Andy knew, as well as they did, that he didn't need to answer to them. He was a man, on his own. But the utmost respect that he had for the man and woman who raised him to be a man, would be there for the rest of their lives. He would answer their questions and reverence the fact that they loved and respected him.

"So…then, the wedding will go as planned," Laura stated.

Andy glanced at her.

"Well, Judd had indicated to Jesse on the phone that…"

"Yes, mam," Andy interrupted her, "there's no reason at all that mine and Summer's life should be held up." Andy was unshakable on the issue of Abigail Luke. What she claimed could easily be proven a lie.

But, despite that, he couldn't help but wonder what, or who, had happened to her so soon after she arrived at college. Her dad had seen that she got there safely. What could have happened after that?

He didn't want to think about this anymore right now. Summer would become his bride in two days. And he would have two small daughters to raise. This is the life God led him to and it's where his heart was. It's where he wanted his thoughts to be for now.

During that night, Andy woke up suddenly from a deep, dreamless sleep. The digital clock on the floor beside his bed read 3AM straight up. That used to be a time the Lord would wake him, and compel him to get up and pray. This was the first time it had happened since before his rodeo hiatus.

He immediately wanted to sink back into that deep sleep, but he forced one leg over the side of his bed, then the other, and slid to his knees next to his bed.

After thanking the Lord for every blessing he could think of and praising Him over and over—he was finally awake and

112

fully enjoying the Lord's Presence. The Spirit of God began a parade of people's faces in a vision for him to pray for. Emma Jo was one of those faces. Abby Luke was another—and he prayed diligently for them both and all the others, before he climbed back into bed and slept soundly.

Laura rolled over to sleep facing her husband and automatically slid her hand across the sheet to touch him. She woke up when his spot was empty. In the nearly black darkness of the room, she could see him sitting on the edge of the bed.

"Jesse, honey, are you alright?"

He half turned and reached for her hand. "I'm fine. I woke up with Pastor Judd on my mind—doing a little praying for him."

"What time is it?"

"About four-thirty. I believe I need to go visit with him."

"Okay, but maybe you should try to get a little more sleep first."

Without hesitation, he slid back under the light bed covers and pulled Laura close. She felt so fragile inside the wrap of his heavily muscled arms. But he knew that was only a physical delicacy she had. Emotionally and spiritually, this little woman had a strength that he stood in awe of.

"I know there seems to be a lot going on, Jess," she whispered, "but, *it will all work itself out*—a wise man once said to me. Well, he said that a *few* times over the years, actually."

"Well...not too long back, you would be popping loose at the seams over Andy's sudden life change, especially as major as this one is. But, these days, life just flows around you and you just let it." He paused a second. "Is that an old age thing?"

"No, it's called learning to keep my eyes on Jesus and trust Him—And who are you calling *old?*"

She giggled when he faked a snore in her ear. "That's what I thought, tough guy."

Jesse had prayed in his private spot in a barn stall, on his knees, before heading to the Double OO to see Judd and Toni. He figured this was going to be a tough conversation, if Judd would talk to him at all.

"Come on in, Jesse," Toni said, as she held the heavy pine door open, but kept her eyes on the floor.

He removed his hat as he stepped inside. He didn't say anything to offer comfort, as he might usually do. He could see her eyes were red and puffy. He'd been around the female species enough to know that any offering would bring on a storm—of some sort.

"Have a seat in the den, Jesse. I'll get Judd."

He settled on one end of the leather sofa, wishing he was as good at *keeping his eyes on Jesus* as Laura was. He had no idea what to expect out of Judd, but he *was* sure that God had this in Hand.

"Jesse." Judd stepped into the den in his sock feet and held out a hand. He sat on the opposite end of the couch from his friend. "I'm glad you came."

He nodded. "I want to be here for your family, Judd. But you need to know that the Lord woke me up at four this morning and made me know He needed me to come see you."

The corner of Judd's mouth pulled in a slight smile. "Well, I asked Him for a way to keep this situation from destroying our two families lives—our friendship. As usual, He seems to be ahead of us on this."

"What do you mean?"

He cleared his throat, his face somber. "Abby came to our bedroom sometime after midnight last night. She admitted to me and Toni that Andy could not be the father of her baby. She said they had never been sexually active. Andy didn't tell me that. I understand now why he didn't say anything. He couldn't. He was caught in the middle between me and my daughter."

Relief flooded Jesse's whole being at Judd's revelation.

"That young man carries a lot of wisdom in his young self."

"Yes…he does. Thank you." Both were silent for a minute. "Judd, what can I do for you and Toni? For Abby?"

Before he could reply, both men were on their feet at the high-pitched scream that came from upstairs.

"Judd! Oh God…Judd!"

He met his wife midway on the staircase—Jesse stopped on the bottom step, his heart in his throat.

She carried a sheet of notebook paper that Judd grabbed from her hand and quickly read. He hurried back down the steps and shoved the paper at Jesse as he ran past him to his office.

Jesse read the handwritten note: *I can't do this. I'm ruining everybody's lives. I'm so sorry. Please forgive me, Daddy. Forgive me, Mama. Forgive me, Jen.*

Ten-year-old Jenny Luke came in from the back patio when she heard her mom's scream. "What happened, Mr. Jesse?"

Toni ran past him toward the office, and met Judd almost head on in the doorway.

"My handgun is missing from the hidden drawer of my desk. She knew where I kept it. Toni, search every closet and small space in this house. I'm heading for the barn."

Jesse squatted down in front of Jenny and worked at sounding calm. "Honey, did you see your sister this morning?"

Judd and Toni both froze, waiting for her answer.

She nodded, not sure what was going on.

"Where did you see her?"

"She rode off on her horse."

"When? How long ago?"

"When I looked out of my window this morning. The sun wasn't up all the way, but I saw her ride out of the barn on Little John. I wanted to ride too, but she was already gone."

"Which way did she head out, Jenny?" Judd was at the kitchen door pulling on his boots, knowing she was several hours ahead of them.

She pointed in the direction of High Point. They all knew that way would also take her into the canyons.

When Toni grabbed up her boots inside the mud room, just off the kitchen, Judd took them from her hand and set them back down. She was crying. He pulled her to him, then and held her a full minute in the tight, comforting wrap of his arms. "Stay here and call Laura Brandon and the others who you know will pray. I'll find her."

Jenny put her arms around her parents and patted their backs. It was almost Judd's undoing. He put an arm around her and squeezed. "Take care of Mama til I get back."

Both men went out the back door. Just as they separated to head different directions, Jenny ran out behind them.

"Daddy! Mr. Jesse! Mama said to wait a minute."

They came hurriedly toward her just as Toni rushed outside. "Laura just called, Jesse. A little girl named Emma Jo is missing from your ranch. She was riding around on one of the kid's ponies and nobody has seen her in the past hour. They can't find her."

The men looked at each other, both realizing these were two entirely separate incidents.

"Head on out, Judd. I'll get Les Kane alerted for you and my boys when I get home." Jesse figured Emma was just being Emma and had managed to kick Poncho or Buddy—more like Poncho—hard enough to get a little ways out of the ranch yard. She'd probably be back at the barn by the time he got there.

Within twenty minutes, Jesse had a posse from High Point spreading out on horseback and in pickup trucks by some of the women. Every direction possible to travel was being covered. Emma was still missing. He watched as an unusually large plumb of dust formed through the back pasture behind the barn and knew Granny Martha had to be behind the wheel of that

116

vehicle. He shook his head and rode out on one of the ranch geldings.

Andy and Beau spurred their horses out of the yard, headed toward the Honeymoon Hideout—the decades old line-shack that had been turned into a cozy little getaway for newlywed guests. Their first concern was to locate Emma Jo while Donny, Hank Walton and Jesse headed toward the canyons, praying they could intercept Abby Luke before she did something she couldn't take back.

As he made his way to a line of timber, Judd knew Abby could have switched directions and headed for the creek and someplace on the back ninety. There were too many fresh tracks mixed together until he spotted the ground freshly kicked up by one horse just as the main path ended. Those tracks led straight into the thicket of the woods. He picked his way slowly to keep from crippling his horse in the briars and dense undergrowth.

He couldn't believe this was all happening. Funny how he was remembering the sermons he'd preached many times about how no one was exempt from sudden disaster, learn to pray without ceasing and keep your eyes on Jesus and spend time everyday reading the Bible and in prayer—And all he could think right this minute is just what good did that do for him and his Bible reading, praying family? How did any of that help the fact that his and Toni's first born was out in bear and wolf country, packing a handgun just big enough to make either of those predators mad enough to kill her and she's already suicidal? He didn't have the faith in himself at this moment to even try to pray—he was mad. Mad at God? Mad at his nineteen-year-old daughter who had been taught better than this all her life? Mad because deep down he felt like his family should have been exempt from these disasters? He well knew better than that, but this minute he was filled with fear. This was his baby out here. He began to crumble inside.

Out loud, he cried, *"God—God, my Father—forgive me. Help me find my Abby. Lord, send angels to protect her. I'm asking in Jesus the Savior's Name."*

He swiped his forearm across his face to get the teary blur out of his eyes. He'd lost any semblance of tracks some time back, but continued.

Abby couldn't remember ever being afraid riding by herself, but she'd never gone so far away from the beaten path between her house and Andy's. She thought she would have found where the High Point crew was working by now. She had to find them soon. It was the only way she could think of to carry out her plan—and she was so lost.

Her parents would be searching for her by this time. She had to get this over with.

Something put Little John on alert suddenly when his ears perked and his body stiffened under her saddle. Then she heard a horse whinny. She had come through two gates and knew she was on High Point land. But she reined in-between a circle of pines and stopped, waiting for a sign of the approaching rider. *He* must have come looking for *her.*

When the head of a small dappled pony came into view, she was shocked to recognize the aged little Poncho. She would know that horse anywhere—Abby was one of several kids that had learned to ride on him. Then, her mouth dropped open when she saw the rider—a very small girl with long dark, big hair.

She moved Little John into the opening and both horses sounded a greeting to each other. She saw that the child had been crying.

"Well, hi. Are you alone?"

Emma nodded. "I got lost."

"What's your name, sweetie?"

"I'm Emma Jo and I couldn't make him stop and he ran, too, but I didn't fall off."

"Wow. You're a real cowgirl!" Abby figured this child was a guest of the dude ranch and somebody was going to be frantic looking for her—probably a lot of somebody's. This was throwing a real crimp in her plans, but she had to get the girl to safety.

"Why are you here, lady? Are you lost, too?"

Abby found it suddenly hard to swallow. What *was* she doing here? Between her and this little girl, both ranches probably had all their hands searching the canyons and mountainside—losing a day's work. She didn't want to scare the little girl any more than she already was. She looked around and spotted a group of wild blackberry bushes. "Are you hungry?"

"Yes, I sure am. Do you have some food?"

Abby pointed toward the berries. "No, but we can pick a few berries to eat."

"Oh, yes, let's pick berries." Emma slid down the side of Poncho so quick and excited, it made Abby laugh. She dismounted, dropping her reins for a ground tie, showing Emma Jo what to do.

Abby realized just then that the heavy burden that had been weighing her down since coming home from college, seemed to have lifted somewhat. In the few minutes she had spent with this kid, she wondered, for the first time, what her baby would be—a boy or girl? Would its hair be blonde or dark, like Emma Jo's? It's—skin color? Not once had she allowed herself to think about the baby in her womb, in terms of it being a tiny human life that she had any responsibility for—until this moment.

She reached out and gently touched the girl's thick, curly strands that were tumbled down her back.

Emma smiled up at her new friend. "You're very nice and you're pretty. What's your name?"

"Abby."

"Abby is the prettiest name I've ever heard."

In the next instant, both horses reacted simultaneously in fear of something only they could see or hear. They both

119

jumped backward and squealed in fear. Abby grabbed Little John's reins and quicker than she thought she could move, unsnapped the saddlebag and pulled out the pistol she had taken from her dad's desk.

Then, she heard it—at the same time the horses jumped away and took off at a dead run. A large black bear entered the small clearing making threatening growling noises.

Abby released the safety, cocked the pistol, held it high over her head pointed up in the air and pulled the trigger. The shot was loud and reverberated an echo seemingly for miles. Everything had happened so fast, she hadn't thought—just reacted. The bear wheeled and disappeared back into thick trees.

Abby was sick with fear, but when Emma Jo ran to her and wrapped thin little arms around her hips, squeezing her with all her strength, a protective sense of *mama* rose up so strong, it took her by surprise.

Quickly she engaged the safety on the gun and laid it down by her foot as she hunkered down to the child's size and hugged her tight. "Don't be scared, Emma Jo. The bear is long gone."

"But our horses are long gone, too," she bellowed into Abby's shoulder.

"They can find their way home and that gunshot will tell people where we are and they'll come get us."

Emma raised up and took a step back, rubbing her eyes. "Okay. Can we still have some of those berries?"

Abby stifled a laugh. Somehow this little girl seemed to be just what the doctor ordered for her. The doom and gloom that had been covering her for weeks like a black storm cloud wasn't there, at the moment, at least.

They gathered enough berries to satisfy their hunger pangs, then, Abby decided they should walk in the same direction she had been riding—Mainly because the bear had gone the opposite way.

Judd jerked his horse up at the sound of a gunshot. Fear swelled in his throat until he felt light headed. *Father, give me strength.*

Even though the shot sounded faint and far up into the timber, he knew Abby had come this way hours ahead of him. He pushed on, wondering if this day would end his world as he had known it? Would changes come for him and his little family that they couldn't survive? Happens all the time to families— He'd seen marriages crumble when a child died or for way less than that. He was supposed to be the spiritual leader of this area's ranching community and far beyond that. His church had grown immensely in the past few years. Oh, he could preach a good sermon and be a real champion of faith—until his household was put to a gut wrenching test. He'd never felt so weak and helpless—so faithless, as he did right this minute. Fear was consuming him. He rode on deeper into the mountain wilderness feeling sick and alone.

Andy was completely bewildered. He'd searched every inch of the creek that ran from the other side of the Honeymoon Hideout cabin. He practically knew every tree and grass blade by name. Most of his childhood was spent playing on this creek and the surrounding area and it didn't appear that Poncho or any other horse had been back here. He searched for Emma's little footprints, but finally circled back to the ranch yard.

Summer was holding Rachel, waiting for somebody to show up with Emma Jo.

Granny Martha and Laura had made every trail the old pickup could fit on and was standing beside Summer, trying to comfort her. When Andy and Beau rode back in empty handed, Summer couldn't be still any longer.

"We're heading up toward the timberline," Andy announced as he and Beau attempted to keep moving on past the women, but Summer wasn't having any of it.

"I'm going with you, Andy. Get me a horse to ride."

"You need to stay here with Rachel," Andy said. "We'll find her and…"

"Don't tell me what I need, Andy Parker. I *need* to find my baby and Rachel can ride with me." Anger and fear interlaced her tone.

Granny Martha stepped forward and took Rachel from her. "Now, you go mount up behind Andy. I'll see after this baby."

Without hesitation, Andy instructed her to put one foot in the stirrup and throw her other leg over behind the saddle as he pulled her up in one solid yank. In seconds, they were moving, Summer's arms wrapped tightly around Andy's waist.

"Andy! Beau! look!" Laura pointed toward the field headed out to the Cowboy Church. Two saddled, but rider-less horses trotting side by side, sweaty and blowing, headed for the ranch yard. They all recognized Poncho. Laura immediately stepped in front of them, her hands and arms up to bring them to a stop.

Beau dismounted and quickly examined each one for bite or claw marks or other injuries, which he didn't find.

Andy exchanged glances with his mom. "That's Abby Luke's horse, isn't it, Andy?" she asked.

He nodded, "Little John." Confusion coated all their faces.

"I'll take care of them. You boys go on." Laura gathered up reins while they rode out in the direction beyond the church— toward the mountains. Now, they knew they were looking for a couple of girls on foot, not horses—however to pete this even managed to happen!

By the time they reached the thicker part of the woods, navigation became slower. Andy fully expected Summer to go hysterical on him by now. Instead he just heard her calmly praying against his back—some words he understood, other times she prayed in a spiritual language of other tongues.

"They came right through here, Andy." Beau pointed at the ground where dirt areas clearly showed horse tracks.

"Abby! Emma!" Andy shouted and they stopped and listened. Silence. Again, he called their names.

"Hey," a man shouted from the trees not too far away.

In minutes, Judd Luke appeared. "Andy, Beau, I'm sure glad to see you boys." He nodded at Summer. "Mam." He removed his straw Stetson long enough to rake an arm across his forehead and replace it. "Abby's on Little John out here—somewhere. Have you seen any signs?"

"Actually, Little John and Poncho came running to our place just a little bit ago. They looked like they'd been running a long way." He pointed his thumb behind him. "This is Summer Logan. Her five-year-old daughter was riding Poncho around the yard this morning and disappeared. The tracks of both horses ran right through here. So, it looks like we're hunting two girls who are afoot."

Confusion crossed Judd's face and Andy just shook his head. "All I can say, Judd, is they ought to have quite a story to tell when we find them."

"I heard a shot that came from higher up quite a while ago. Abby's got my pistol with her."

Andy nodded and without another word they headed for higher ground while Summer began praying again.

Jesse, Donny and Hank had ridden the far end of the canyon edge, finding no tracks or any signs that Abby would have been there. But what they *did* encounter was Clint Berry, one of High Point's hands that Donny had hired a few months back. When he'd heard the story, and was asked to help in the search for Abby Luke, he figured what she might be up to.

He had met her about a week ago when he was doing day work for the Double OO. She had ridden out to the back ninety and seemingly singled him out for a little flirty conversation. She wanted him to help her get to the Jackson airport when she decided to go. He told her where he would probably be working on certain days and agreed to drive her to wherever she needed to go. After she rode away that day, he didn't expect to see or hear from her again.

"I guess she remembered that I would be up in the higher pastures working today. She didn't seem too sure of herself when she asked me to help her. That's why I just sort of blew the whole thing off."

Jesse was relieved to hear Clint's story, knowing she was not suicidal. But why on earth would she want to disappear like that?

"Clint, I'm just curious now, mind you," Hank leaned forward over his saddle horn where he could fully see the man he was talking to, "but, if that child had found you out here and asked for a secret ride to Jackson, would you have done what she wanted?"

Clint raised up straight in his saddle and lifted the split reins on his horse's bridle in an up and down motion. He stared at his hand movement, thinking about how to answer that. Finally, he looked up at the older gentleman, who he had come to fully esteem. "Hank, with all due respect and as honest as I can say it, I never once thought of her as a *child*. She told me she was almost twenty, but her state of mind at any given time would have been a factor for me. I can't rightly say what I would have done until I was faced with it."

Hank's expression never changed. He just nodded his head and remarked, "Good enough."

The group headed across the foot of the tree line, venturing further into the thicket for a couple miles. It was getting late evening and soon it would be cooling off considerably.

Jesse was getting worried that they hadn't run across Judd yet. He tried to reach him on a two-way, but either he had forgotten to bring it or it wasn't turned on. Every so often they stopped and called for him, then Abby. There was no answer. Hopefully he had found her and was long headed for home.

It rankled him that in this day and age, there wasn't any way to communicate. Cell phones were useless here. At least every man was on a good strong horse and armed to the teeth.

"Abby, I want my mama." Emma began to cry for the first time all afternoon. Most of the day, they had walked without talking. She kept figuring that any minute they would run on to something familiar or someone out looking for them. Her sense of direction was zero and that didn't help. At any rate, Abby couldn't let her know how petrified *she* was or how bad she wanted to see *her* mama's face right now.

Just up in front of them, she saw a shallow cave with a large overhang of rock. "Emma Jo, look up there. Wouldn't that be a great spot to rest. We could pretend we're cave-dwellers—just until someone finds us."

"But, what will we eat? And I'm thirsty, too," she wailed.

Abby took her hand and pulled her up the last few steps to the clearing. "I'm thirsty, too, but when my daddy or your daddy comes to rescue us, they'll bring water. Let's just sit under here and rest til they get here."

With the side of her boot, Abby scraped an area of the ground from the rock wall out about six feet and they sat side by side against the wall.

"What's your daddy's name?" Emma asked.

"Judd Luke. He's a preacher."

Emma sucked a surprised breath and broke a smile. "My daddy is a preacher, too, Abby. We're like sisters, aren't we?"

She laughed at that. "Maybe so. What's his name?"

"Andy Parker. He asked me and my baby sister if he could be our daddy because we don't have one anymore and my mama is going to marry him."

Abby felt like ice water had been thrown on her at little Emma's words. She was staring straight ahead in frozen silence until the girls' voice broke through her breathless trance.

Peggy Patrick

"I betcha Andy comes to get us because he always does that. God sent him to our house up on the mountain to rescue me and Rachel and Mama from our fire. It burned up our house and now we live at Andy's cabin. But he won't sleep there yet cause he has to marry Mama first, Mama said. We all got brand new dresses and shoes, too, for Mama's wedding and now I get to call Andy, Daddy.

Abby heard every word Emma said in her nonstop way of telling all she knew, but strangely, the thing that sounded louder than the rest was her simple—*God sent him to our house.* It seemed that everybody around her gave God Almighty all this credit for their life's happenings.

"Why...do you think God *sent* Andy to your house, Emma Jo?"

"Well...because he got lost in the dark and got in a storm and found our house, but he slept in the barn and his horse did, too."

"Did he say that God sent him to your house?" She didn't know why this was so important to her, but she felt such a strong need to understand.

"Yes, he did and Mama said that, too, because we were all out of food and Andy had some in his truck and orange juice, too. And when we had a storm, the angels came and carried Mama in their big arms and laid her on top of me and Rachel so we didn't get the house falled on us."

"Angels?"

Emma Jo looked up into Abby's eyes and in her wiser-than-her-years reasoning, and with great sympathy, she stated her question, "Abby, you don't know about angels. do you?"

She shook her head, "No."

"Well...do you know God? His real name is Jesus."

Abby was suddenly thrown into a disturbing need to know what this little girl was talking about. It didn't make sense. She had heard of Jesus all her life—Listened to her dad preach about Jesus and she'd learned to say prayers to Jesus—but—*angels*

126

carried her mother? Why did this even matter to her? It didn't mean all that much before. This had been one very long trying day. She was overwhelmed and exhausted and scared out of her wits. That's all it was.

"How about we get some real rest and try to sleep, Miss Emma Jo. They'll wake us up when they get here."

"Okay. Can I lay my head on your lap?"

"Sure." She helped her get comfortable, knowing she wasn't going to be able to sleep. It would be dark in another hour and—she didn't want to think about it.

"Abby?"

"Hmm."

"We forgot to say our prayers."

"Okay. Do you know a prayer?"

"Well...I think we should do the praise dance first." Emma jumped up and pulled on Abby's hand. "Come on. It's fun and God and the angels will watch us dance."

The last thing she wanted to do was stand up again right now—never mind *dance!* This child was so full of energy and wild imagination. But, she figured humoring her with a little dancing around was better than giving her too much time to feel her thirst and hunger.

Slowly, Abby got to her feet and Emma immediately began to twirl around with her arms raised high over her head.

"Like this," Emma instructed, "and then we praise Jesus loud enough so He can hear us all the way to Heaven." Then she shouted, "Praise to Jesus! I love You, Jesus," and she twirled and jumped and danced around, flailing her arms all around.

Abby forced her arms up about half way and turned in a circle a couple of times, but she couldn't force the words out of her mouth. The foolishness of it was too much. She sat back down and watched Emma Jo enjoy her little burst of childish energy.

Finally, she sat back down, too, and within two minutes, fell asleep with her head in Abby's lap.

When full darkness blacked everything around her, Abby kept her hand on the handle of her pistol that lay on the ground beside her and fought with every cell of her being to not give way to panic. She wanted to pray, but who would hear her. She had never believed in her father's God. She just went through the rituals of attending all the church functions and singing the songs along with the church congregation. She said the memorized prayers her daddy and mama had taught her, as far back as she could remember. And right this minute, she wished she could believe that all that God stuff was true, because she had never felt so scared and alone.

"Up here, Jesse!" Judd answered the call of his name that was shouted from the near darkness. In minutes, the riders met up.

When Jesse and his group saw Summer on the back of Andy's horse, looks of confusion and squinted eyes were exchanged. It was getting cold and no one was dressed for this kind of night up on a dark mountain, especially Summer Logan. Thin white slacks and a short-sleeved blouse wasn't going to be pleasant up here.

Jesse felt irritated at Andy for not thinking better than to bring her into a situation like this—until Beau filled them in on the fact that Emma Jo was lost, too—"Both horses those girls were riding came running into the ranch yard. They were winded and wet. We're figuring and praying they're both together."

"But, whether they made their way back home by now," Jesse added, "or headed off the wrong..."

"Listen! Shush!" Summer quieted everybody and strained to hear. "That!" She shook Andy by his shoulders from the back. "Did you hear it," she whispered at a near squeal?

"I sure did. It was faint, but I caught it." Andy said.

"What did you hear?" Judd strained his ears to catch whatever it was.

"My baby—she's shouting praise to God. Probably dancing, too. I heard her voice." Summer roughly patted Andy's back. "Let's go, Andy. She's up there somewhere in the dark!"

"I didn't hear a thing," Hank said.

"Me either, but my hearings not as good as it used to be." Jesse tried to sound positive.

"Well, I sure heard it," Andy said excitedly. "We're going to have to pick our way in the dark. They're up there." He wheeled his horse around to face them all after reaching around behind him with one arm to steady Summer. "Let's pray right now. We're going to need extra help to get through here in the dark."

Hats all came off at once and as Andy prayed and asked God to lead them straight to the girls, Summer interlaced his prayer with praise to the Lord, out loud.

Judd felt the power of those two young people's prayers flood through him until he had to get a grip on his saddle horn.

"Let's ride," Andy shouted right after his amen.

Shafts of moonlight filtered through the trees intermittently, but it was enough to keep the posse moving.

An hour later—Andy called the girls names again for the twentieth time. They stopped to listen—and this time, an answer came back!

"Daddy? Emma, wake up. They found us."

Judd dismounted and ran to grab Abby into his arms.

Summer had slid off the back-end of Andy's horse and ran, dropping to her knees in front of Emma Jo. All three females were sobbing—the cowboys stood on the ground holding their horses, swiping at a few loose tears and letting the reunion have its full moment.

***

CHAPTER TEN

After the emotional reunion had settled, Hank Walton took his hero's bow when he produced a gallon sized baggy of slightly flattened biscuits and a canteen of water from his leather saddle bags.

Emma Jo ran to be first for a biscuit and a drink, clapping her hands and squealing at the sight of the feast in Grandpa Hank's hands—drawing chuckles from the relieved search party.

After the two girls had their fill, the remaining biscuits were passed around along with the canteen. "When did you have time to pack food and water, Hank? —Or know it was needed?" Jesse handed him back the near empty canteen.

"Your wife ran it out to the barn when I was saddling up. She knew something."

Jesse nodded and grinned. "She *always* knows stuff. My little bride's hot line to Heaven was lit up, as usual."

It was unanimously agreed that they would wait out the night there—start back for the ranch at dawn.

Clint and Donny scouted around and hauled in several rocks to circle for a campfire and plenty of dead wood to get it going. The horses ground tied with their saddle girths loosened, having been promised a beeline for the creek first thing on the way home by Andy.

Summer sat up against the wall and cradled Emma's head in her lap while she slept.

Abby insisted on Judd's shoulder for a pillow. Hank picked up the revolver from the ground where she had left it with the safety unlocked. He locked it and handed it to the pastor. Judd had a lot of questions for his daughter, but none that wouldn't keep.

Everyone else found a suitable spot until daylight, except Clint Berry. He insisted on keeping watch all night, refusing Andy's offer to take a shift. "I'll keep a fire burning. Don't need any four-legged visitors getting too curious."

Andy sat down beside Summer and draped his arms around her and Emma Jo to help keep them warm the best he could. "You okay, baby?"

"I am now. I don't think I've ever been so scared in my life—scared of losing one of my children."

"Do you realize that it was Emma's praise to God you taught her that caused us to find these girls?"

"I was just thinking about that. We have to praise dance with our children, Andy, every day so they will never forget. I'll always love Joe for teaching me about Jesus and about praise." She glanced up at Andy, not sure if what she said was appropriate now that they were getting married. "Is that all right to still think about Joe sometimes?"

He kissed her forehead. "You're always going to remember Joe. You were his wife and had two babies with him. You worshipped the Lord together. He was your first love—And it's all right to hold on to that memory. When he could no longer take care of you and his babies, God had me waiting in the wings to step in."

She snuggled closer against him and wrapped an arm around his middle. "I love you so much, Andy, I could just burst."

He smiled and whispered close to her ear, "Thank You, Jesus, for giving me this beautiful woman to love." In moments, they both slept.

The trip home began at the crack of dawn. Everyone had slept off and on, Clint still refusing to share the watch. He already had the horses ready to be mounted and the fire ashes cold by the time the group was on their feet.

"Berry, I'll have to serve you up a double portion of gravy and biscuits for the next week, " Hank quipped. "I, for one, appreciate your diligence watching out all night. The others began to express their thanks, but he waved them off and mounted up to ride drag.

Emma Jo clapped her hands with joy when she was invited to ride home behind Grandpa Hank. "Got any more of those biscuits, Mr....Mr. Grandpa?" The way she looked straight up into his face, so seriously hopeful, caused his heart to melt nearly to liquid. But it was the *Mr. Grandpa* that did him in.

He dropped down to one knee in front of her with all the seriousness he possessed. "Baby girl, you can have all the biscuits you want as soon as we get home. But, if you won't tell anybody," he reached into the pocket of his thin leather vest and pulled out a small round biscuit, "you can have this very last one from yesterday.

Her eyes grew as she took it from him. "Well, would you mind if I told just one of us?"

"I guess that would be all right." He stood up, curiously watching her.

Carefully, she halved the small bit of bread and went to Abby. "Here," she said and handed her half. "You had to get rescued too, so you're as hungry as me."

Her logic was sweet, but her generosity was purely sacrificial. The whole group were silenced at this child's willingness to share her tiny morsel of food when she was hungry. Andy saw Summer smiling broadly at her daughter and he couldn't have been prouder of her if she was his own blood.

Hank mounted up, then Andy swung Emma Jo up behind him. Abby rode behind her dad.

It was late-morning when the weary hungry riders reached the High Point barn. Laura, Granny Martha and Toni Luke literally ran to greet them, hugging Emma and Abby as if they'd been gone far longer than overnight. Toni and her daughter shed tears and gave long hugs, letting all questions and explanations be silent until later.

"Soon as the horses are taken care of," Laura announced, "Martha and I have a huge pot of stew and biscuits and cornbread ready for all of you. Come on to the house."

Summer was exhausted to the point of nausea and the pain in her upper legs was too much to stand any longer. Tears began to run down both cheeks as she leaned against the horse Andy had just pulled her off of. Until this moment, she hadn't let on how miserable she was.

He dropped the reins and instantly scooped her up in his arms and headed for her cabin.

Hank and Jesse watched him go, then exchanged knowing glances.

Clint Berry moved silently past them and took Andy's horse inside. He unsaddled, groomed and put hay and grain in the stall that Hank pointed out to him.

Abby and Emma Jo had been herded to the house by the women and when the men were ready to go to the house, they realized Clint wasn't there and no one had seen him leave.

A small four-man bunkhouse was pulled in on wheels and set up on the far side of the ranch about three years ago. A pen and shelter was built off to the back of it for horses. Clint lived there and at present, he was the only one.

Neither Jesse nor Donny were particularly surprised. Clint had proven himself to be a bit of a loner since Donny had hired him a few months back. Beau Vance had worked closer with him than anyone on a daily basis and spoke highly of his ranching knowledge and abilities. The other day-work cowboys that came out from the surrounding area seemed to get along with him, too. There just wasn't a whole lot known about him. His background check was clean and Donny had liked him well enough when he met him in Gillette. But they remembered how standoffish Beau was when Andy first brought him to the ranch. Maybe Clint just needed a little more personal attention. Jesse made a mental note-to-self to ride out and visit him at the bunk house first chance. Right this minute, that stew and a large chunk of cornbread was calling his name.

As he entered the kitchen door, Granny Martha nearly ran him over on her way out with a container of stew and baggy of biscuits and cornbread in front of her face.

"Whoa there, Granny girl." He caught the bread before it hit the floor and balanced it on top of the covered bowl. He knew exactly where she was going without asking. "I'll be happy to take that up to the kids for you, Martha."

"Nope. I got this. You sit yourself down and eat. I need to check on that little girl—get some food in her and make sure she's going to be all right."

"If Andy needs help, let me know."

Andy twisted the knob, then booted the door open. He'd refused to put Summer down until he got her inside the cabin. He knew full well the pain she was in after straddling his horse for hours two days in a row. The fact that she held it all in until they got home was a testament to the sheer strength of this woman. And the fact that he didn't even think about what the long ride was doing to her until she nearly collapsed at the barn, made him know that he was far from the man he needed to be. He should have watched for her welfare better than this.

She was still crying when he gently laid her on her bed and carefully stretched her legs out. He pulled off her shoes and went to the bathroom to draw a hot tub of bath water and searched unsuccessfully through the cabinet for some pain medicine. He'd have to run up to the ranch house and get it while she soaked in the tub.

He turned the water off and heard light rapping on the open front door. He peered around the corner to find Granny Martha waiting in the doorway.

"Granny, come on in." He was happy to see her face right then, being a little unsure of himself in this situation.

"Don't mean to butt in—I just brought you and Summer something good to eat."

He rushed over to take the container and bag and set it on the kitchen bar.

"Is she in the bath tub?"

"Not yet." He motioned for her to follow him into the bedroom, figuring Summer might need a woman with her right then.

Granny Martha leaned down and patted her arm. She was still crying and knowing all she did about this young girl, Martha had to use restraint to keep from wrapping her arms around her. "I want you to eat the stew I brought. You're about starved. Can I do anything for you before I go, honey?"

"No, thank you so much," she whispered with trembling lips.

"Your girls are taken care of today, so you just rest now."

Summer nodded and smeared her hands across her face, feeling a fresh wave of sobs rising. "I'm...sorry. I don't know why...I...can't stop crying."

"Well, I do and you're justified in doing it. You've got a lifetime of pain to wash out. I figure this physical pain you're in just sort of pulled the trigger."

When she turned to leave the room, Andy was behind her and intercepted her exit with a quick, tight hug. "Thanks, Granny."

"Here." She reached into the pocket of her apron that was tied around her waist. She pulled out a couple packets of pain reliever and a bottle of rubbing alcohol. "You know how to use these. You take care of her. You've done a really good job taking care of her whole family up to now." She patted his shoulder, and left the cabin.

Without a moment's hesitation, he went to the kitchen for a glass of water and set it on the wall shelf beside the bed. He grasped her upper arms and without a word, gently brought her up to sit on the side of the bed. He ripped open a packet of the pain medication and gave her two capsules with the glass of water.

"Swallow these, Summer—then I've got you a hot bath to soak in for a few minutes. By then, you should start to feel better and you'll be ready to eat something."

She downed the medicine and wanted to lay back down, but Andy pulled on her arm to coax her up at the same time he set the glass back on the shelf.

"Come on, sweet lady of mine. I'll help you. Let's get this done so you can go to bed."

She stood and crippled her way to the bathroom. Andy closed the door behind her and went to the kitchen to dish up some lunch for both of them.

Thirty minutes later, Summer emerged wrapped in a full-length white terry bath robe and walking stiffly, but better.

Andy heated the stew in the microwave and they both ate like tomorrow was canceled.

"I had no idea riding a horse would do this." She glanced up at Andy where he was seated on the opposite side of the bar.

"I'm sorry I'm being so much trouble." Tears began to spill over again and he went to her and silently helped her up and then back onto her bed.

He sat on the edge of the mattress and placed his hands on the bed on either side of her head. "Summer Logan, don't you ever think for a minute that you are trouble for me. And don't ever think that shedding tears is wrong."

She covered her eyes with her hand and began to weep again, but he continued.

"You're going to be okay, baby. You stretched muscles that don't get stretched that way and they're just mad and yelling at you for it."

He smoothed tendrils of damp hair away from her face and pushed long curly strands off her shoulder. Looking at her tear-stained face, the pain he could see in her eyes and had glimpsed so often when she was sitting alone with her own thoughts—he breathed deeply and felt a heavy thankfulness that she was laying in this bed at High Point, that he had been led into her world so he could hold her and love her—help her find a wholeness that she'd never known. Tomorrow he would bring her fully into his world, into the new home they had designed together and—into their bed.

"Granny Martha was right, Summer," he whispered and kissed her forehead. "These uncapped tears are carrying a lifetime of pain. Don't hold them back and don't be ashamed of them. God's just washing your sweet little soul. I love you, more than my own life, angel baby. I'll help you through this—me and you together."

She put her arms around him and he wrapped her up in his, pulling her into him. He held her tightly, silently for a long time.

Her weeping had stopped and he released her, knowing she was beyond exhausted, needing a long sleep. Just as he was about to go and give her a few hours to herself, he remembered the rubbing alcohol.

After he explained the necessity of a rub down to her, she was too tired to respond other than a simple, "I can't."

She had a big day coming up tomorrow and he knew how much better it would go if—He took the bottle from the shelf and sat beside her on the bed. Her eyes were shut and she appeared to be dozing off.

"Honey, I'm going to rub down the upper part of your legs. Are you listening?"

"Yes. Thank you." She untied the robe, keeping her eyes closed and let it fall open.

It was a full twenty seconds before he could take his eyes off the most beautiful sight—her body, still covered, but barely. The silk sleeping shorts and fitted rib knit sleeveless T fit her slight little figure so perfectly. All he could think was *God is so Good to me.*

Forcing himself into an all business mindset, he gently, but thoroughly massaged her muscles from her thighs down to her toes. About midway through, she covered her face and began to cry—so silently, it broke his heart. He continued until the rub down was the best he had in him.

When he finished, she was asleep. He pulled her robe loosely back around her, prayed for God to give her a peaceful sleep, then left.

On his walk back toward the ranch house, he thought about how different today could have turned out. The dangers that lurked on that mountain where the girls had traveled was too much to dwell on—but he also knew that the number of angels that encircled them was much greater. In his mind's eye, he could *see* the angels dancing and rejoicing along with Emma Jo as she did her praise dance in the middle of the mountain's dangerous enemy territory. He smiled at the thought. His mind was mixing the human side of events with the spiritual side— and then it dawned on him. *This* will preach! God had just rolled a message into him that he had to deliver. He also felt like it was the Lord's way of telling him it was time to step back into the pulpit. A pull of desire had already gripped his heart and he knew first hand, when God puts a calling on your life, He doesn't take it back—but encourages you toward fulfillment.

He entered the barn and went around to the back row of stalls to check on the ranch horse he had been riding. He figured someone would have taken care of the tired, hungry sorrel, but double checking his animals was second nature. Finding the gelding well taken care of—even brushed down, mane and tail included, Andy was impressed and a little surprised. Under the circumstances, that part of grooming would normally wait til later.

By the time he made it to the house, Jesse had the smoker fired up for the wedding reception brisket and chicken. Grandpa Hank was in the kitchen whipping up his famous cookie dough and a stack of Laura's white table cloths set in the middle of the island bar.

"What's going on, guys? Somebody getting married or something?"

"Oh, Andy," Laura came into the kitchen carrying another small stack of the tablecloths, "how is Summer doing?"

He raked a finger through the dough bowl when Hank turned his back and slurped a big glob into his mouth. "She's asleep now, but I'm going to stay down there with her tonight. Her emotions are so raw and that saddle nearly took her down. I'll need to take care of the girls so she can concentrate on resting."

"That's what Granny Martha was telling me. Andy, do you think she'll be emotionally ready for this wedding tomorrow?"

He nodded slowly as he gave her question serious consideration. "Yes, I believe she'll be better in the morning, Mom. Just be sure we keep everything simple. She's as anxious to get our lives started and into a routine as I am. Our girls need that. And…speaking of…where *are* the kids?" He turned a circle. "*Any* kids?"

Laura laughed. "Your kids and mine are with Uncle Donny and Aunt Reeny. They'll all be back here for the night. I've already fixed for them so why don't you take care of Summer tonight and I'll handle the girls."

He looked at her and nodded. "Thank you, Mom. I appreciate all this help...and understanding. It means everything to me."

"I know it does, honey. We all need help at times and understanding. And some of us need a whole lot of both."

He stepped to her and wrapped her up in a bear hug. For the first time, he realized what a tiny little woman he had for a mother. Why hadn't he noticed that he no longer looked up when he talked to her. Maybe the size of her heart and soul overshadowed her short stature.

"Unhand my woman, cowboy!" Jesse came into the kitchen from outside and popped his hat onto the peg by the door.

Andy released her and turned to his dad. "Hey, I know who bakes my cookies around here."

Hank turned half way around toward him and snorted with great offense.

"Uh–oh, I'm messin' up." He hurried around the center island and grabbed Hank in a tight hug from behind. "What I *meant* to say was, I know where the best spaghetti and stew is made. but as for the cakes and cookies—Grandpa here is my hero." He gave the old man a quick squeeze and reached for another glob of dough from the bowl he was holding.

"Kid, if you want weddin' fixins' made by tomorrow, you better get outta my kitchen."

Jesse and Laura both laughed as Hank swiped at him with a batter-sticky wooden spoon.

Andy danced a jig toward the back door." "I'm going— Right now!"

"Hey, how is our girl doing?" Jesse asked with all joking gone.

"Sore. Emotional. But she'll be all right. Thanks, Dad." He started out the door, then stopped and turned partially back around. "Where's Beau working today?"

"Double OO—restringing fence that old Sourdough pushed down. If you ask me, that bad bull needs a trip to a good rodeo stock company. More trouble than he's worth."

"I agree with that. I'll be at the Double OO for a few hours while Summer is sleeping." He went out and headed for his pickup, hoping Les Kane had a pony left in the pen he could ride to the back ninety. He knew that's where the fence was down. A few hours of day work sounded like Heaven right now. He'd missed the camaraderie with the cowboys, especially Beau. These day-workers were a different breed of cowboy than a lot of the rodeo riders he'd met on the circuit, although that certainly wasn't true of all of them. But, these High Point and Double OO hands were noncompetitive, some family men, but all willing to go the extra mile for each other or a stranger when called on—not trophy-buckle or championship minded. This was home and that meant more to him now than it ever did. He was glad for his rodeo experience, mainly because it gave him a new sense of what was truly important in his life.

He parked among the several dually's at the Double OO barn and got out. Judd's truck was under the awning at the front door. He hadn't talked to Judd about Abby's situation since he'd been confronted at home a few days ago, although he did know from his dad that she had told her parents the truth—that the baby couldn't be his. He stepped inside, into the alleyway, hoping he was still welcome here.

"Andy." Judd stepped out of the tack room. His expression was strained, but not angry.

Andy thrust out his hand and Judd took it and pulled him into a short man-hug, patting his shoulder with the other hand.

"I was about to leave to come find you—to apologize. I was way out of line with you. I'm…I'm truly sorry."

Andy hated the sadness that filled his pastor and friend's countenance. "I understood, Judd. There's no hard feelings here. How is Abby doing, if I can ask?"

"She was sleeping when I left the house. I don't have any answers to all this yet."

Andy nodded and hesitated a moment. "Well, sir, I'm not real sure if this is appropriate to ask you, but...any way you would be able to do a simple wedding ceremony for Summer and me. If not, I fully understand."

"When?"

"Tomorrow evening in the pavilion."

"Yes, sir, Andy, I would be honored. Thank you."

"Your family is invited. Just family and friends from our ranches here. Grandpa and Dad are cooking brisket and the trimmings. We just want to say *I Do* and eat. Nothing fancy."

Judd smiled, thinking he had never seen such wisdom coming from someone so young. "I'll pass the word for you."

"Thank you. Hmm, would you have a mount for me. I thought I'd go help pull some wire."

"Yes—" He turned to glance down the isle of the barn. "I believe the gray is down there. He could use some exercise."

"All right."

"See you tomorrow." Judd went out and got in his truck.

Twenty minutes later, Andy stepped up in the saddle and as he exited on the opposite end of the barn, Abby stepped into view, startling the gray—then Andy.

After a few seconds, the gelding decided nothing was going to eat him and Andy stepped down.

"Abby? What...are you doing down here? Your dad just..."

"I'm not looking for Dad. I saw your truck pass the house earlier. I was hoping to see you."

"Abby..."

She put a hand up. "Don't say anything. You don't have to." Tears gathered and she wrapped her arms around herself. "I needed to tell you how sorry I am." She swiped hurriedly at the

142

spilled tears. "I…just don't want you to hate me for what I did. For what I said about you." She hesitated, glancing at the ground, then back at him. "I told Mom and Dad the truth…that the baby wasn't yours."

"I knew you did. Is there anything I can do to help you, Ab?"

She looked down again and slowly shook her head. "No." Her tears had stopped and a hardness sounded in her voice. "No," she repeated. "I need to see someone else. Do you know where I can find one of your ranch hands named Clint?"

"Clint Berry? Not this minute, but he lives in the bunk house on the far north acreage. He could be there catching up on some sleep. But he'll be there by dark, anyway. Do you remember where that is?"

"Yes, thank you—And congratulations on your upcoming marriage. She's very pretty."

He felt uncomfortable. "Thank you."

"No…I mean it, Andy. I'm truly happy for you…and for your new family. Emma Jo said God led you to rescue them. Do you believe that?"

He couldn't help but smile. "I do believe that."

She stared at him for several seconds, wondering, pondering how it must feel to believe something like that. "I wish you all a happy life together." She stepped to him and reached her arms up to hug him. He tightened his free arm around her back and for only a second, she felt a twinge of regret. She wanted to say *I love you,* but turned and walked away instead.

Abby knew she could get to the bunk house by driving most of the way. It was almost dark when she parked her car just inside the north gate into High Point property. The road wasn't more than a washed-out cow trail from this direction that led to the hand's quarters, so she parked and began walking the quarter mile or so through a section of woods. She was as familiar with this area as she was the High Point ranch yard. She and Andy had ridden their ponies through these woods many times pretending to be outlaws or mounted police—whichever struck their fancy that day.

She told her mom she had a very important errand to run, promising to be back in an hour. Against Toni's better judgment, she loaned her the car. But, Abby had no intention of messing with her mom's trust. She had destroyed enough in that department to last a long time.

It was a beautiful evening and she was surprised that she was even noticing. A cool breeze ruffled the cottonwoods high above her, filling her senses with a strange peacefulness—She couldn't remember ever feeling anything quite so precious—so perfectly calm.

Clint Berry. He had seemed like such a nice guy. So respectful. He'd taken off his bent up old straw Stetson when she began to talk to him out on the range that day. Who does that? For *her*. He'd looked at her like she was someone special. His face had turned a shade of pink beneath the darkness of his suntan and work dirt. She hadn't meant to embarrass him in her desperation to disappear—run away to where no one knew her and leave with nothing but the clothes on her back. How foolish that seemed now. She still had no answers to her dilemma, but something caused a change in her thinking—suddenly.

Five-year-old, Emma Jo, had seized a prominent place in her mind and her heart. That little girl's prayer dance seemed so silly at the time, but she couldn't get the image of those little arms and legs jumping and twirling every which way and—her voice—she could still hear her voice saying *I love You, Jesus,* as loud as she could shout.

She was so deep in her thoughts, the lights of the bunkhouse surprised her as she rounded the last curve in the trail. The sight of it jerked her rambling thoughts back to what she had come here to do.

As she approached the railing of the porch that ran the full length of the oblong log cabin, she could see Clint through the uncovered window. He was sitting at a small picnic styled table reading a book under the light of a table lamp—the only light that broke up a too dark night.

Before she could reach the gate opening to the porch, she heard a low menacing growl coming from just behind the front door. A glance back through the window caught Clint on his feet with a pistol in his hand. He reached for a rifle that leaned against the wall behind where he sat and propped it against the table. He was squinting, trying to see into the darkness out the window.

Her feet froze to the spot just steps from the house when she heard the growl again. Then the only light went out plunging the whole area into blackness. Her heart jumped straight up her throat and pounded hard.

The dog didn't know her and it could attack before she had time to make Clint know it was her out here. *Oh, please don't let the dog out!* She wanted to cry out, call Clint's name, but when she opened her mouth, a raspy illegible sound came out.

Suddenly the door opened just a crack.

"Who's out there. I'm locked and loaded. Better make yourself known."

"Me. Abby." This time her voice was almost a squeal.

The dog barked a warning through the door opening.

"Sit, Sara Lou. Sit."

The porch light came on as the door opened all the way. Clint stepped out and went to her. It was clear she was traumatized. "Abby? What in blazes are you doing?" He glanced around. "Where's your vehicle?"

She pointed behind her. "At the north gate. I…left it there."

His eyes grew as he turned them back on her. "You walked here from *that* gate. It's nearly a half mile through the woods."

"I didn't mean to scare you."

He still had his revolver in his hand, but clicked the safety and stuck it in the back waist of his jeans. "This is how people get shot, Abby. Or dog bit." He fought to keep the anger he felt from hurting her feelings, but realized he'd failed when she covered her face and began to cry.

He reached out and grasped her shoulders. "I'm not mad at you. You just scared the bejebbers out of me because I had a loaded gun aimed your way and a dog waiting for a signal to take you down. And it's so dark tonight."

He caught her hand and squeezed gently. "Come on inside and let's begin this visit all over again. You can tell me why you came."

He led her by the hand and squeezed gently. "Come on inside." When the dog whimpered she couldn't see, but she dropped her free hand down and felt the pup's cold nose touch her.

The table lamp was clicked on and she saw the most beautiful blue merle Aussie with kind, accepting eyes—one blue and one brown.

"Abby, meet SaraLou. SaraLou—Abby."

She kneeled and wrapped her arms around the dog's neck. "You're so beautiful, Sara Lou."

When she stood and looked up, Clint was gazing at her, his eyes twinkling with a smile. It gave his countenance a whole new look—soft and sweet.

"Come sit down. Do you drink coffee?"

"Yes, thank you. Black."

"Whoa. I would have pegged you for a cream and sugar type."

"Nope—I learned to drink from a thermos of strong black coffee riding out with my dad on cattle roundups when I was about ten."

He laughed. "I hear that."

He sat on the bench across the table from her and moved the book he was reading aside. She couldn't help but notice it was a Bible.

"So, Miss Abigail Luke, what brings you out here this dark night?"

She sipped her coffee and set the cup down before looking him straight in the face. "To apologize to you."

He stared straight back at her. "Why?"

"For...trying to involve you in a ridiculous scheme...of helping me run away."

"No apology is needed for that."

"Yes, it is. That could have turned out to be an ugly mess for you...with my family and even here at High Point."

"Well, I'm a big boy, Abby. But I am glad that things have been straightened out for you."

He doubted things were actually fixed for her. He watched her stare into her coffee mug, looking as if she had more to say. "Abby, you're safe with me." He spoke softly.

Her gaze went to his face again and she couldn't—didn't want to look away. She needed a friend right now, but not sure about giving up her darkest secrets to a virtual stranger. But then, maybe that was a safer bet.

Clint wanted to comfort this girl. He could clearly see her mind was heavily burdened and probably had everything to do with why she felt so compelled to run away from her family. But here she was offering him an apology for trying to involve him—and she was still needing his involvement—somehow.

"Abby," he wanted to reach for her hand, but refrained, "you can talk to me if you want to. We don't know each other, I know, but I'd like for that to change."

She continued to stare at him, desperately wanting to talk to him—to trust him.

"Do you want to tell me why you were running away?" He had the urge to go around the table and hold her. He knew so much of the time, these crises felt a lot larger than they were.

"I was going away to get an abortion." Her voice was even toned—her expression one that said she was braced to be thrown out of the bunk house. But, it was a relief just to say the words.

He knew how to keep a stone face when hearing or viewing something shocking, but that was the last thing he expected her to say. All he felt was an intense compassion and greater urge to go to her. She's carrying a baby!

"I...guess the baby's father doesn't want it?"

"No. He doesn't want it."

"Have you changed your mind, then, about the abortion?"

She nodded.

"You know, Abby, I could clearly see how much your dad loves you. Is there a problem with you staying home with your parents?" He was trying to get her to open up and talk to him. "How is your mom taking all this?"

"I think they'll both be all right with it. It was a shock to them. I just don't want to put the financial burden of this baby on them, but I don't have any options until I can get through this and go to work somewhere."

"Well, I *did* hear a conversation a few months ago from Judd Luke that his super smart daughter was planning for law school. So, you should have enough knowledge to know that you can force the baby's father to pay support."

Abby's hand shook so hard suddenly, she sloshed coffee all over the table. "Oh!" She stood and he knew he'd hit a nerve hard. Her face flushed and tears filled her eyes. "Not always, you can't"

"Why?"

"Because..."

"Because why not?"

"Not if you don't know who he is..." Her voice rose to near hysteria, "or *what* he is!" She slapped a hand over her mouth, realizing what she had blurted out—The worst deep, dark shameful day of her life! "Oh...oh!" She turned and headed for the door, yanked it open and ran.

Before she got out of the clearing, Clint caught her by an upper arm and held her until she stopped struggling to get loose. Then he simply pulled her to him and wrapped both arms tightly around her. Her sobs were ripping his heart. She immediately relaxed against him and allowed this tall, tight-muscled cowboy to keep a crushing hold on her—wishing he would never, ever let go. His strength felt like a safety net with steel sides—like nothing could get through to hurt her again.

As long as she needed him to hold on to her this way, he would stand right here with her. What she had just revealed was soul shattering for him. He could only dare to imagine the pain inside *her* young soul. God in Heaven! —She was raped!

Anger besieged him as he allowed his mind to form those words. He pressed his hand to the back of her head, then back down to massage her upper back. He said nothing, but let the security of his embrace soothe her until she stopped crying. When she stirred, he released his hold and she took a step back.

"I...don't know what to do now." She shook her head. "I don't know."

"This was a horrible thing that happened to you, Abby. And some day when you're ready, I want you to tell me the whole story. I'll help you all I can." He cupped her face with both hands. "Listen to me. You did nothing wrong. Nothing! And regardless of how this happened, that's an innocent human being growing inside of you—a tiny little baby that has purpose the same as we all do. God loves us all, no matter how we started out."

"God?" A flash of anger consumed her and she backed up out of his reach. *"God* does *not* love everybody. Where was He when those monsters...those..." She began to cry again, but when he reached for her, she slapped at him and began to scream.

Easily and as gently as possible, he scooped her up in his arms and carried her back inside. Sara Lou began to bark, but he silenced her with one word.

He put Abby's feet on the floor, but she collapsed. He promptly went down with her—Then she began to scream and scream until there was no breath left in her. As hard as it was to hear that kind of pain coming up out of her, he knew it was a good sign. She said *those* monsters. Dear God! He vowed then and there to find out whatever he could—where and who was involved.

After the screaming subsided, she lay in his arms crying. He picked her up and carried her to a bunk that had clean bed coverings and lay her down. She went into a fetal curl and continued to softly cry.

"Abby, you're safe here," he whispered close to her ear.

He went into the kitchenette on the other end of the building and picked up the phone. After a lengthy conversation with Abby's mother, Toni, he poured himself a fresh cup of coffee and let SaraLou out for a potty run. He sat outside in a rocker, sipped his brew and asked God for His mercy and His brand of peace for Abby Luke.

He didn't reveal to her mom that her daughter had been raped. It wasn't his place to reveal that and certainly not on the phone. She did agree to letting her sleep where she was unless she chose to come home later. Either way, Clint promised to not let her out of his sight until she was safely back home, whether tonight or tomorrow.

Having that kind of trust from the Luke's was a special thing to him. They had gotten acquainted through Cowboy Church services and more so by working alongside each other when he hired out for day work on their ranch. He had felt drawn to the Luke family right from the start of hiring on for High Point. They were a ministry family for Jesus Christ, but it seemed that most of the people on both ranches were spiritually inclined—people of prayer.

Maybe if he had known about God the way he does now, his world would not have been blown apart three years ago when a home invasion took his family. And he worked in law enforcement, keeping the townsfolk safe. While he was out doing that, the thieves and murderers broke into his own home and—

SaraLou trotted over and with a small whimper, stuck her wet nose in Clint's hand. He rubbed his hand over the side of her face, then down her back. She seemed to catch the direction of his thoughts. She and Lynn Berry were best buds.

"I miss her, too, sweet girl."

But who could say that God would have changed what happened. Christians were killed—murdered every day. At least he had the comfort of knowing that his wife was a believer in Jesus when she died, even though he was not, and their son, who would have been born that Christmas went into Heaven with his mom.

***

CHAPTER ELEVEN

Clint leaned back and pushed his long legs out in front of him for a needed stretch. The evening couldn't get more perfect—It was a good time to sit up and watch for Abby, in case she woke up and decided to head out in the middle of the night.

He remembered the first year after Lynn's death, he had turned vigilante and cleaned out the gangs in every back alley he could find. He'd gone a little nuts—until the Chief demanded his gun and badge and forced, what turned out to be, a permanent vacation.

The second year, he wandered from place to place working odd jobs and hating everybody that looked his way.

Occasionally, childhood memories would surface, offering slight relief. He had almost literally been born in the saddle—his mom being the dedicated cattle driver on his family's five thousand-acre Wyoming ranch. He was the first born of the Berry clan—born in the pasture grass when Maggie Berry thought she had plenty of time to finish the calf roundup after her water broke. She was more careful—a.k.a. being threatened within an inch of her life by his dad—with his two brothers and two sisters that followed the next few years.

Those memories always made him grin—made his heart feel happy, every time he thought of it. He'd heard the story told so many times with a little variation here and there, depending on which family member or cowhand was telling it. But it was always funny.

Two of his uncles, his dad's brothers, had made careers in law enforcement. It had always intrigued him and somehow, he chose that for himself over ranching. He left home for the police academy when he was twenty-one.

When he met Lynn at a Christmas party that same year, his whole world became complete. They married a few months later and Clint, Jr. was due on the same day they had met a year earlier.

But it was during the third year after the murders of his family that he was sitting on a park bench in downtown Gillette, Wyoming, not far from his family ranch, when his life took another major turn. A cowboy with spurs jangling, walked up to him, reached to shake his hand and introduced himself as Sonny. He was dressed in the familiar wranglers, a red chambray shirt and looked like he had been in a dust storm. His clothes didn't look odd to Clint, but a little out of place in this part of town. It hadn't dawned on Clint how homeless and dirty *he* looked. He'd been in the same thin ragged jeans and pullover T-shirt for days—even sleeping in them in the seedy little room he'd rented a block away. He had become a bum.

Seeing the young cowboy stirred something inside of him that he thought was long dead—a longing to ride and throw a rope and work alongside of his dad and brothers on the ranch.

He had called his mom once a month to let them know he was still alive, but lied about his circumstance and where he was.

"Hello. Sonny. Clint Berry."

"Mind if I sit a while."

"Plenty of room. Have a seat."

Sonny sat down on the small bench.

Clint turned his head half around looking one way then the other. "Where'd you tie your horse up at?"

Sonny laughed. "I left him in the barn—drove here."

"Why?"

"That's what I'm wondering."

Clint straightened a little and cut his eyes sideways at the young stranger. "What do you mean by that?"

The cowboy looked at the ground in front of him and rubbed his palms back and forth on his upper legs. Then he clasped his hands together and leaned forward, legs apart. "Well, sir, here's all I know. I was working my young colts this morning—got bucked off twice, too, by the way—when I suddenly get this strong urge to get off my horse and get on my knees and pray. So, I tied up little Rooster—that's my favorite two-year-old filly—"

"Rooster is a *filly?*"

"Yeah, she makes this noise like—well, anyway, so I kneeled down right there in the dirt and thanked God for the day and asked Him if He was needing me for something. I waited about a minute and I was pretty sure He spoke inside me and said to drive over to Gillette and speak to the man sitting on the bench. So—I drove here and saw you and here I am. So, what can I do for you?"

Sonny tilted his head around to look at the man beside him. He had no idea when they had started, but tears were running in dirty streaks down Clint's face. Finally, he lowered his head and covered his face with both hands—now his shoulders were shaking with his sobs.

"You don't know our Savior, Jesus, do you, Clint?"

He shook his head, his face still covered.

"Do you want to meet Him while I'm here? He sent me to town just to find you. You're lost in your sin, man."

Clint sucked a deep breath and smeared the wet dirt across his cheeks. "What do I do? Help me."

Sonny put an arm around the shoulders of his broken, new friend, told him the Gospel story and then, led him to Jesus in prayer. Clint Berry asked God to forgive his sins and clean him up. At the end of that prayer, both men began to chuckle—then laugh out loud. They both laughed like a couple of drunks—but finally when that subsided, Clint jumped up and smiled ear to ear. "I feel it! I feel like shouting! I feel alive!"

Sonny stood and hugged the new born-again child of God. "You *are* alive. You have just been born into the Kingdom of Almighty God. Go ahead and shout and holler all you want to, dude." His grin was as wide as Clint's.

SaraLou whimpered and put a paw up on Clint's lap. That memory had triggered laughter and tears anew as he relived the most life altering moment he'd ever had.

"I'm all right, SaraLou. Everything's fine."

He had attended a church with Sonny for a few months afterward, remaining where he was until deciding to go back home.

But, some friends of Sonny's—Donny and Reeny Brandon—attended the church in Gillette one weekend. Donny mentioned he needed to hire a good hand at his ranch and without thinking about it, Clint asked for the job, was hired on and here he was.

And there lay a young, scarred woman inside his cabin, needing somebody to let her know she was beautiful and worthy. Had God sent him here—for her? He had contacts in law enforcement and he fully intended to get that ball rolling in her situation. But, there was something besides that. She had singled him out of a dozen wranglers on the back ninety of the Double OO asking for help that day. And she came to him tonight. But he hadn't been able to get her off his mind since the moment he'd laid eyes on her the first time. He'd never prayed for anybody so intently as he did her when she was lost up on the mountain. And right now, he knew it would break his heart if he never saw her again after this night. He didn't care that she was carrying a baby because of a rape.

"Clint?"

He jumped at the sound of Abby's voice calling his name. He spilled his cooled coffee on the porch at his feet, splattering his pants legs. He set the cup down and hurried inside. When he got to her bedside, she was still sound asleep. Was she dreaming about him? Was she calling for him to save her from a nightmare?

"I'm here, honey," he whispered. He pulled a quilt up over her jean clad legs, leaving her tennis shoes on her feet.

After bringing SaraLou in and cleaning up his spilled coffee, he sat on the floor beside Abby's bed and rested his head on the edge of the mattress. After a few seconds, he felt her hand reach for him. He covered it with his long, warm fingers and both slept soundly.

Andy felt like a new man—albeit one who had been run over by a Mack truck. He was tired beyond belief after several hours of pulling fence wire and wrestling with a cantankerous old bull who wanted to jump in everybody's back pocket. After the full day and night he'd just spent on the hunt for two lost girls—he stopped by his parents' house, showered and packed supper for him and Summer and headed up to spend the night in her cabin.

Despite his exhaustion, he felt a thrill at the idea of spending a few hours alone with her. Just one more day and nothing would separate them—day or night. Their new house was ready and mostly furnished.

Summer had been adamant about not wanting to go away for a honeymoon. The idea of moving into their new home felt like a honeymoon to her. But, Andy decided a trip somewhere—just the two of them, would be more exciting for her as a first anniversary present. By then, she'd be settled in and things would be getting familiar—losing a little of the fresh excitement. But then again, with her, maybe not. He wanted to give her the world—the moon. He knew he couldn't love her more than he did this minute.

The cabin was dark when he went in. After a quick check, it looked as though she hadn't moved since he'd left her hours earlier.

He dished up the supper he'd brought onto paper plates to heat in the microwave. In ten minutes, with two smoking plates in hand, he wheeled toward the bedroom—And stopped dead in his tracks at the sight of Summer standing in the doorway of the hall watching him.

They made eye contact before he let his eyes roam from her face down the skimpy T-shirt and shorts she wore. He could tell she enjoyed every second of it and he couldn't help giving her the enjoyment. He set the plates on the bar without taking his eyes off her, then stepped to her, stopping when there was no space left between them.

He stroked her long thick hair, finger brushing it back from her face and shoulders.

She smiled up at him, her eyes lit with that unmistakable love light.

"I'm glad to see you're feeling better."

She reached and pressed her hand to his chest. "I think it was the rub down you gave me, except…"

"Except what?"

"I'm just a wee bit still sore. Maybe I should have another rub…"

Before she could say more, Andy's mouth was on hers. She instantly responded, returned the kiss until she could feel his heart about to pound out of his chest. Or was it her own heart running away with itself?

She heard him groan as he wadded her hair in his hands and kissed her like a man on a mission. For her, his kisses always felt like the first time she'd truly been kissed. She'd never been held by a man the way Andy held her...when she was hurting, when she cried and like now, when he was wanting to make love with her. What they were experiencing together this minute—the ache, the joy, the fire of desire that surged like an electric current through their young bodies—left them both gasping and needing.

When he raised his head, and looked into her flushed face, he knew he *had* to stop where this was headed or neither of them would be able to.

"Whoo—woman!" He touched his forehead to hers, reluctantly fighting to force his pounding blood veins to simmer down. "You're going to make me lose my mind!"

"Oh, Andy." She ached with a need to be wrapped in his strong arms—an overwhelming need for fulfillment in his bed. But tomorrow night would be all the sweeter after they were married. They had discussed this and both agreed to wait to come together sexually until they knew it was right with God, too. Just one more night alone and it seemed like that was too much to ask. A fire was blazing *now*.

"I know, baby. Lord do I know." He stepped back and took his hands off her. With his hands clasped together, he cleared his throat and turned around. "Okay then, my *almost* bride. How about we eat!"

They sat across from each other at the small bar that jutted out from the wall dividing the kitchen from the den and ate without talking until they finished.

When his eyes found hers, he didn't believe for a second that Heaven could get any closer to earth than this. This woman was beautiful and she loved *him*. She was about to take his name in a few hours. Would she always love him? Could he make a woman like her happy for a lifetime?

As she gazed back into those dreamy, sexy and so gorgeous eyes that were filled with love for her, she vowed silently at that moment to be the most loyal and loving wife she could possibly be—Not because he had rescued her and her babies and given them beautiful things—But, because he was Andy Parker and she believed the sun itself rose and set inside his being just for her enjoyment. She didn't want to be separated from him another night—another minute.

"Stay with me tonight, Andy," she said softly. "Your mom is keeping the girls all night."

He nodded slowly. "I know. I planned to stay here. I thought you would still be too sore to get around, but…"

"Oh…but I am still *sooo* sore. That rubdown is about to wear off in about five minutes, I'd say. I'm going to need another one…immediately."

He tried to keep his spreading grin to a minimum as he got up, stepped around the bar and took her hand. "Come on, I'll help you hobble back to bed and we'll commence…uh…with the rubdown."

She held on to his arm and put on a terrible act of *can't hardly make it.* "See, I'm already stove plumb up," she whined, then chuckled.

Andy's boyish grin broke into a laugh. "*Now* I see what I'm in for…Lord, help me!"

It wasn't until a few minutes later when he began to massage the inside of her upper legs that she yelped and jumped in intense pain. "Not there. Don't touch me there." She was choking back tears suddenly. He moved to flip on the big overhead light and forcefully turned her where he could look at the area of her leg that was too painful to touch. His eyes got big when he saw the blackish–purple and blue bruising on the inside of both her legs. He was silent for a long few seconds. He knew her pain was mainly from being saddle–sore, but didn't realize the severity until he saw this. He laid his hands on her hips and so gently smoothed his fingers down her outer legs while he whispered a petition to the Lord for healing.

"I'm sorry this happened, Summer. I didn't realize how bad you were bruised."

"I'll be okay. It looks worse than it is."

He bent over and touched her lips with a feathery light kiss—surging her tears again. "I don't believe that. You don't have to put on a brave front with me. These bruises are serious and I'll be here to take care of you tonight."

He left her to rest after getting her to swallow some pain caps, figuring thirty or forty minutes for them to begin working.

He cleaned up the few dishes in the kitchen and locked the cabin door. A phone call to his mom to check on Emma Jo and Rachel—Get the basic schedule she and Granny Martha had planned for the ceremony tomorrow, along with his own plan, then quietly pulled off his tennis shoes and laid on top of the covers beside Summer. His black sweat pants and white short sleeved T-shirt was a little more than his usual sleeping attire, but this wasn't a usual night in bed for him.

Summer's light, steady snore told him she was asleep. He stretched out on his back and without allowing his thoughts to get too heavy with the little beauty beside him, he slept.

Andy walked out the kitchen door of High Point Ranch headquarters—the ranch house he'd grown up in—and knew it was the last time he could call it *home*, at least in the same sense he'd done for nearly two decades. Walking beside him was his best man—his mentor—his dad since he was five years old. Jesse Brandon was his hero. He had hugged his son close just moments before heading out the door to join the rest of the family and guests.

Andy knew he'd never forget his dad's words after he'd hugged him. *"Andy, remember what you said to me just after*

*your mom and I were married? You said—'Hey, Dad, I'm your
boy now.' I need you to remember when you have your own boy
running around—you'll still be my boy."*

Jesse swallowed hard as he walked beside his *boy* to stand
in his honored place as his best man.

As the two men approached the pavilion, about twenty
people stood in two groups making an isle down the center of
them. Jesse and Andy were directed by Reeny where to stand
and immediately Carly Vance turned on a tape of the wedding
march.

From somewhere behind a group of tall flowering cactus
emerged Donny with the most gorgeous woman on his arm,
turning the waiting groom's knees nearly to liquid. Her hair was
brushed back from her face, long and blowing in the slight
breeze. She was dressed exactly like he would expect—a simple
yellow and rose print ankle length dress with little cap sleeves
and a V-neck. A garland of silk wildflowers graced her head for
a veil.

Immediately behind Donny and Summer came Grandpa
Hank with two little girls—identical mini-replicas of their
mother, from the dresses to the hair garlands. They walked on
either side of Hank, one on each of his arms.

Donny handed Summer over to Andy and Hank left the girls
standing on either side of their mother.

When Andy squatted down to face the girls, they both
giggled and hugged him. After pledging his forever love to each
of them, Jesse handed him two little bands that he placed on
their tiny fingers.

"Oh, Mama, look. I'm pretty," little Rachel squealed in
delight. The crowd laughed with her.

Both girls remained beside Summer as she and Andy turned
toward Pastor Judd and spoke their vows.

The evening was joyful—lots of laughter and storytelling.
Finally, Andy and Summer Parker dashed out to their dually

through a shower of bird seed and cheers, and headed off a few acres away to their beautiful new cabin for a night of wedded bliss.

MawMaw Laura excitedly took her two little instant granddaughters home for the night.

Judd Luke was the only one from his household to attend the wedding. He was gladly obligated to do the honors for Andy and Summer—but something was waiting for him at home that didn't feel right. In fact, he couldn't shake the dread that had come over him when Clint Berry followed his daughter home only minutes before he had to leave for High Point. He had excused himself as soon as the short ceremony was over. Abby had something she needed to say and they were waiting until he returned home.

Before he entered his home, he sat in his truck and prayed—*Lord, I ask You for the peace that surpasses understanding over myself and my family right now. I don't know what this is about, but You do know. Take charge of this—because I'm sure I'll handle it all wrong without You. I'm receiving Your peace over me and my family now just as You taught me to do according to Your Word in Hebrews 11:1. Thank You, Father, in Jesus Name—*He remained still and focused on his Heavenly Father until he could see with his inner vision a golden hue settling over him and then each member of his house. When he got out to go inside, he felt feather light and unnaturally calmer with each step he took. He had indeed received the peace he had just asked for.

He found his wife and daughter seated together on the couch in the den and Clint across from them in a winged back chair.

"How was the wedding?" Toni inquired before he got seated in a matching chair next to Clint.

"Nice. Very simple, but a God ordained union, I fully believe."

"That's wonderful. Abby has something she needs to tell us. She's asked Clint to be here."

"All right." Judd looked a little surprised at that, but had no issue with Clint Berry. He was one of the hardest workers he had doing day-work and he regularly attended his Cowboy Church. "Abby, what is this all about, honey?"

Abby gazed over at Clint as if to summon some extra courage from him. He nodded his head, urging her to tell her parents her story.

"I'm going to just say this bluntly, Dad, Mom—because I don't know how to make it easy. Let me say the whole story while I can get it out."

Judd and Toni exchanged glances, brows furrowed, but waited quietly.

Abby's emotions, thankfully, seemed to be under control. "I don't know who my baby's father is. I don't even know if this baby will be white, black or brown."

She felt both of her parents' tense, even though they remained silent. She refused to look at either of them as she continued talking. "The first week at school, I was blind folded and driven to a party where they were hazing freshmen. I went believing it was just all in good fun." She hesitated a few moments, continuing to stare at the floor in front of her. "I was raped...more than once. I never saw a face. Their faces were covered from the time I was picked up. I heard someone else crying, but I don't know who she was. I was driven back to my dorm late in the night, still blindfolded and left standing on the sidewalk. I tried to shove down my emotions and go on to my summer classes, but I couldn't concentrate." She paused a moment. "When I realized I was pregnant, I came home. I decided I needed to leave here and go someplace else. I randomly picked Clint to ask for a ride to Jackson airport because I planned to have an abortion. I went to his place last night to apologize to him and I guess I had a meltdown. He took care of me and convinced me to tell you the truth about…about everything."

Judd blinked droplets from the pools in his eyes. His gaze remained focused on his daughter's easy, placid expression—a look on her face, that was now lifted up toward him, that he'd never seen on her before. Her eyes were—smiling?

When his gaze went to his wife, he could tell she was seeing something very different in Abby, too.

No one spoke a word for several long moments. Judd thought he should be ranting and racing to get at the scum that did this to his little girl. But—God was in this room with his family. His peace was softly settled on everyone, just like he had asked for. But, there was something—more. Something about Abby he couldn't define.

Toni's eyes were sparkling with unshed tears. She thought she should cry, scream out in anger at God for allowing this horrific thing to happen to her child—and yet, she somehow had known that Abby was hiding a terrible secret. A mother's instinct, maybe. She seemed to have been prepared to hear this.

Clint broke the silence. He leaned forward with his hat in his hands. "Abby told me some of this story today. I've already taken the liberty of getting a couple of private investigator friends of mine to find out what they can about these men. They've both been in law enforcement for a long time and know how to get information they want."

Judd gazed at his daughter. "Why couldn't you tell me or your mother this when you first got home? Did you think we wouldn't help you?" Judd was clearly hurt and frustrated that this private information had been trusted to one of the ranch hands—And a virtual stranger, at that.

"I never intended to tell anyone, Dad. It just…happened. You were so angry that I dropped college and then that I was pregnant. I couldn't find a place to tell you. I'm sorry, but you were so disappointed in me—and I felt so dirty and..."

"Oh God, Abby." He dropped his head down and covered his face with his hands.

Toni sat still, swiping tears from her cheeks—knowing Abby and her dad needed to have this conversation. There had been an underlying strain between them for a long time—years, but she'd always chalked it up to Abby being a teenager. But, did it have to take something so ungodly cruel?

"No, Daddy, Mama—listen to me. There's more. There's something else I have to tell you." She stood up then . "I don't blame you, Daddy. *You* didn't make me feel that way. I...I met someone. I met a man...today. Someone you both know well, but I had never met him." She stopped and looked at Clint. His smile reassured her, encouraged her to keep going. She sucked in a deep breath. "I never knew...your God, Dad."

Judd and Toni both turned shocked eyes on her at the same time.

"I heard you both talk about God all my life, but I never believed He was real. It all sounded so foolish to me. Today, Clint prayed with me and I asked Jesus Christ to forgive my sins and save me. And..." her face crumpled. "And He did. I can feel Him."

Judd stood slowly to his feet, the shock on his face deepening. Toni got up too, as Abby turned toward her. The women shared a tight hug, both with tears streaming.

"You knew, didn't you, Mom?" Abby asked through her tears and joyous laughter.

I knew you didn't understand about the Lord, but I prayed for you every day and I knew God would find a way to reach you."

Judd broke out of his frozen shock and reached for his daughter. He pulled her to him and held her tightly for a long minute while they both cried.

Clint stood and put up a hand to Toni to stay where she was. He quietly circled behind the seating area and went out the front door. The Luke family needed privacy at this point and he had a decision of his own to make.

He headed back to High Point to put in for an extended leave of absence. He was going to join forces with his friends in the investigation of Abby's attackers—No matter how long it took, he would find them.

Clint stopped by the Double OO a couple days before he would be leaving the state. He didn't want to just disappear without letting Abby know. Plus, he wanted to reassure her that he would do everything in his power to bring justice to her and her baby. They both, at the very least, had that coming.

When Abby swung the front door open, the sight of her standing there in a sleeveless black and white, high-waisted, floor length silky dress, her blond hair hanging loose, it took him a few seconds to find his voice. She was messing with his heart and the odd thing was, he didn't mind.

"Hello, Abby."

The deep gravely sound of her name spoken out of the gorgeous lopsided grin that stood at her door, nearly stopped her heart. "Clint."

The satisfied surprise on her face told him the attraction he felt toward her wasn't one-sided.

"Please come in."

"Well, I thought maybe you'd like to sit outside. It's sure nice out here."

She thought if he had just asked her to run off to the farthest end of the earth with him, she'd go. "Okay." She went out and they settled into the porch swing.

"I just want to make sure you were doing all right after the other day. That was a traumatic time you had."

"Thank you for helping me through all that and I'm fine, thanks."

"I'm glad I was here to help you."

"I'll be staying here at home indefinitely, until after the baby comes. It's like Mom said, 'One day at a time.'"

"You have a very wise mom."

She nodded and smiled, "She's actually talking about fixing up a nursery. I think she's excited about the baby."

"I can understand why. This is *your* baby, Abby. Her grandchild."

"Dad hasn't said much since…that day I told them everything."

"He'll come around. This is *his* grand baby, too"

She stared at the porch floor, silent for a full minute, then said, "I…heard you were leaving." *Please deny it.*

"I have to. I've taken a job with a private investigation firm in Nebraska. I promised you I would find out who attacked you. I meant it. I'll be back in touch, but I have to say good-bye for now."

She hesitated a moment before putting her hand on his knee. Immediately, he responded by taking her hand and sandwiching it between his large, warm ones. His fingers closed gently around hers.

"I'll call you and we can talk all you want to." He reached into his shirt pocket and pulled out a small folded piece of note paper. He held it out to her and she took it with her other hand." I was hoping you would want this. It's my cell number. You can reach me day or night."

She smiled and nodded, but her heart was breaking at the idea of him being gone so far away. He didn't feel like a stranger to her anymore. Far from it.

"Abby," he whispered, as he put an arm around her and pulled her close against him. "I'm going to miss you, too."

She looked up at him and he lightly grasped her chin and kissed her trembling lips.

Five Months Later

Carly hadn't ventured much farther than her own front porch for the past month. For one thing, she was too big now—eight and a half months along with her twin boys. Feeling exhausted was the norm the past weeks, but on this beautiful sunny day, she went on a cleaning binge that would have made Martha Stewart proud. Every nook and corner in the house sparkled and glowed like brand new.

By the time Beau got home that evening, she had showered and dressed for bed, then fell asleep curled up crossways on top of the still made-up king bed.

He ate supper at Hank's chuck wagon every evening, then brought home an extra plate for his miserably pregnant Carly.

He set her supper carton on the kitchen bar, his eyes roaming around the walls and floors and furniture—not sure he'd ever seen the place looking and smelling so spiffy. Surely, *she* didn't do all this.

When he found her curled up on her side, both arms cradling her extremely extended belly, he could only lean against the door frame and watch her sleep. She was his whole world. The fact that she was willing to put herself through all this—carrying two tiny little boys inside of her all these months—his sons—was humbling to say the least. What had he ever done to deserve this life with this woman? And now, these children—his own flesh and blood with the woman of his dreams.

He tried to be quiet, getting undressed and into the shower.

When he got back, she had gotten up and pulled back the covers on the bed, but continued to stand beside it looking a little unsure of something. She looked like she wasn't fully awake.

"Carly, are you going to get in bed?"

"I can't."

"Why?" Even as he asked, he rushed around to where she stood—a puddle was on the floor between her feet.

"I think my water just broke."

Just as it dawned on him what was happening, another gush of water splattered to the floor. He raced into the bathroom, grabbed a bath towel and threw it on the tile floor. "Step on this, baby. Don't slip down."

She stood on the towel as he grabbed a clean, dry, warm gown and underwear from her drawer.

"Looks like we're having some babies tonight," he said, surprised at his own calm demeanor. "Are you having any pains?"

She shook her head. "No, not yet."

"Put these dry clothes on. I'll get your coat and shoes and get your bags into the truck."

"Shouldn't we call Jesse and Laura?"

"I'll call from the hospital," he yelled as he went out to pull the truck to the front door.

In five minutes, they were headed for Jackson Hospital.

"Mama?" Abby whispered inside her parents' bedroom door. It was 3am when she was awakened by a sharp cramping in her hips and lower back. In a few minutes, the pain came again. She felt scared and could only think of getting to her mom.

"Mama?" She whispered again just as another lower back pain nearly took her to her knees.

"What? Abby?" Toni turned her bedside lamp on at the same time her feet hit the floor.

"What is it?" Judd raised up and raked a hand down his face.

Toni reached for her daughter where she stood on the top step of their sunken bedroom to help steady her until the pain let up. "When did this start, Ab?"

"Just now. It woke me up."

Judd reached for his jeans in the same motion that he sat up and touched his feet on the floor.

Toni settled Abby in a straight-backed chair close to the front door, then ran upstairs. She shoved Jenny's bedroom door open. "Jen, get up and dress. We're going to the hospital with Abby."

All were loaded into the dually within minutes.

"Five minutes flat, ladies," Judd announced. That's a record, *and* I might add—one I'm going to remember," he quipped as they headed around the corner of the drive toward Les and Kaitlyn Kane's home to leave Jenny. It had been prearranged for Kaitlyn to help Jenny get off to school if this should happen during the week.

"Oh gosh, I forgot to call and wake the Kane's up." Toni popped herself on the forehead.

But oddly enough, Les was standing on the porch when they rounded the tree line in view of the house.

Jenny jumped out and Judd rolled down his window. "Headed for the hospital, Les. What are you doing up at this hour?"

"Can't sneak up on this crusty old cowboy. I heard that dually *whining* this direction in my sleep. Tell Ab we're praying all goes well." Les waved them off and followed Jenny inside.

By the time Abby was wheeled into labor and delivery, an hour and a half had passed. Judd and Toni entered the cafeteria to grab a couple cups of fresh coffee and were stopped in their tracks at the table of familiar faces.

"Andy? Donny? Reeny?" Judd was startled, then concerned at who they were all here for.

"Hey there, neighbors." Andy responded, equally surprised. Seeing their questioning faces, he added, "It's our boy Beau. He's in labor. Carly's back there...you know...helping out."

"Oh, the twins are coming," Toni exclaimed. "How exciting! We just brought Abby in, too."

"Well, get some coffee and join us. It's a waiting game at this point," Donny said.

In about thirty minutes, Toni left the cafeteria to check on her daughter. No one had ever asked any questions about Abby's baby's father—nor has anyone treated her any differently than always. She and Judd were both grateful for that.

As she stepped off the elevator, she stopped in the middle of the hallway after recognizing the tall, thin cowboy beside the doorway of a small waiting area. His new looking silver-belly Stetson was in his hands. Standing there in his starched white long-sleeved shirt tucked into new dark denim jeans and dress boots, he would have been unrecognizable, but that timid, lopsided grin and thick light brown wavy hair was a dead giveaway.

"Clint Berry. This is a surprise." Toni offered her hand. "How did you know we were at the hospital?"

He shifted his weight from one foot to the other. "I...well, last time I talked to her, she asked me if I would come back for the birth of the baby. I promised I'd try—so when she called me this morning, I caught a last second flight."

"Well, then she's going to be one happy girl to see you." She stepped to him and patted his back. "Thank you, Clint. They have her mostly out of pain now. I'll show you her room."

He followed her down the hall and as he stepped inside with a rap of his knuckles on the open door, Abby immediately reached her arms out to him. He tossed his hat onto a chair and walked over and bent down into her arms. He hoped no one else came in behind him, but regardless, he was here for this woman. He'd promised her he would try to be. But, more so—he *wanted* to be here with her. Not since Lynn had he felt the slightest draw or desire for a woman in his life, until now.

Each time he had hung up the phone from listening to her voice, he had to pour himself into his investigation work to keep from rushing back to Wyoming.

Abby's case had been completed with justice still in process of being served. Soon that would finish. He'd taken on a couple other cases for his friend's firm, but it was only to keep his brain fully in gear and off Abigail Luke.

Abby lifted her chin and searched his eyes that were twinkling fast and bright. "Stay with me, Clint. I know I can get through this just fine, but I *want* you to be in delivery with me—if you can handle it."

For the second time, he touched a warm, slow kiss on her lips and smiled, "I can handle it. I'll see what I can do. Meanwhile, you better use this time to rest. You might need your strength later." He turned and bent down slowly to pick up his hat, then left the room to go have a conversation with Judd and Toni Luke.

By one o'clock that afternoon, two little boys lay side by side, all swaddled and ready to see mom and dad. Beau was a little white around the gills yet, after standing by his wife's side through both births. They were born three minutes apart, but Carly's extended labor had already taken it out of him. *How do women do this over and over again?* He had some extreme making up to do as soon as he got this orange juice down and got his head out from between his knees.

A pair of familiar boots suddenly appeared under his face— just when he was about to be over himself. *Oh, please, no—not Andy.* He slowly raised up to a sitting position and beat his mouthy sidekick to the punch. "One word—just *one*—and your butt will be tied to the furthest standing tree away from human hearing with the largest ant pile I can tote to the tree! —first chance I get! Comprehend, preacher boy?"

Andy was glad he had thrown his cup of coffee away and didn't have a mouthful right then. He would have been washing the hospital wall. He stretched his lips, sucking them half way into his mouth and bobbed his head up and down in rapid succession. Then he sat down beside his friend and took pity on him.

"Congratulations, cowboy. Two healthy, handsome baby sons. Twice blessed."

"Thank you. I don't think it's sunk in yet."

"Nope, but it will soon enough. I'll call the ranch and let mom and dad and the rest know all is well."

"Okay. I better get back to Carly. That woman's got a strength I can't even…"

"Hey…they *all* do. That's why God gave the birth pains to them. It would kill us dead." Andy slapped Beau's knee. "Hang in, buddy."

Beau and Carly were busy getting acquainted with their tiny bundles when Judd stuck his head inside their room. "We got us a little grandson. I haven't seen him yet, but I'm told he's healthy and looks like me." He chuckled with pure joy as they both gave excited congratulations.

When Judd called the Kane's phone, he asked for Jenny to give her the news first. "We've got us a tiny baby boy, Jen. You are officially an aunt."

"Oh, Dad. Oh…" she began to cry and handed the phone to Kaitlyn.

"Congratulations, Grandpa."

"Thank you, Kaitlyn. I hope those were happy tears."

"Yes, I'd say they were. She just ran out headed to the barn to tell Little John he's an uncle."

They both roared with laughter.

It was an hour later when the Luke's entered Abby's room to get the first close up with their first grand baby. Clint was still wearing his gown over his clothes and his mask was hanging around his neck. Seated beside Abby's bed, he held her hand as the baby slept soundly in his bassinet.

***

EPILOGUE

The phone call only lasted a couple minutes, but it was a satisfying moment for Judd Luke. He left his home office and found his wife and two daughters gathered around the play pen—oohing and ahhing at two-month-old baby David, who was just discovering he had a voice. He was heavy into oohing right back at them.

"Jenny, could you do a big favor for your old dad?" Judd pleaded with a snarky grin.

"Sure."

"Hop on the four-wheeler and run out to the barn. Make sure I closed the hay room door. If anybody on four legs escapes tonight, they'll make a big mess in there."

"Okay." She ran out the back door, always eager to drive the wheeler.

"Ladies," Judd addressed Toni and Abby as soon as he heard Jenny start the engine. "It's over. All four took the plea deal and will serve 10 years."

Confessions had been recorded from four college seniors—all sorry and remorseful for their actions against three young freshmen women that one night—yet the boy's lives were still destroyed along with their families. The senselessness of it all was gut wrenching for Judd and Toni—but justice for Abigail gave them a place to move forward now and be the most fun set of grandparents that God ever let be. They were still young—and running, romping and playing ball was definitely on their extended list of things to do.

Abby didn't look up, but reached into the playpen and ran her fingers through her baby's fine curly blonde hair. She couldn't stop the sudden tears—They dripped onto little David's T-shirt front before she could swipe them away.

Toni patted her daughter lovingly on the back and then went to her husband and wrapped her arms around him.

Judd took his wife's hand and led her toward the back patio to watch for Jenny. He stepped back inside and peered around the door into the den. "Oh, by the way, Ab, I spoke to Clint today while you were out. He just happened to mention that he was coming back to do some *cowboying* for High Point—you know, in case you wanted to know." He winked and went out.

It was all she could do to keep from jumping up and shouting. She had dreamed of this happening over and over, night after night.

Clint had worked for the private investigator's company during these months that he'd been gone—And now, *he's coming back!* But, when? She jumped up and raced to the back door and stuck her head out. "When, Dad?"

"Oh, I think he said tomorrow."

"Tomorrow!" She *did* shout that time. Her heart was about to beat right out of her chest as she ran to call Clint.

She heard her mom giggle. It was stifled, but she heard it.

This was going to be a long night!

****